"Ross, please stop..."

Ross was lying on top of Charlie's sleeping bag, protecting her from the chill of the night. Opening the zipper, his fingers tunneled under her sweater.

She wanted him, but she was afraid. Not of Ross. Of something out there, lurking in the shadows. "Ross, wait!" she cried. "I need to concentrate."

Swearing with frustration, Ross got to his feet and went to kick the fire nearby. "Damn, Charlie! Don't pull that mumbo jumbo on me. If you don't want me to touch you, say so."

"I'm telling you we're in some kind of danger," she said, sitting up.

Ross stared into the fire. "You're so beautiful...but this obsession with the supernatural is going to ruin you."

"And you're a self-righteous hypocrite!"

"*Hypocrite?*" Ross swiveled toward her. "What about you? Leading me on and then panicking and blaming it on a psychic vision...that's contemptible!"

Fuming, Charlie lay down and zipped the bag up to her chin. "I'll see you in the morning!"

Dear Reader,

Back in November 1990, we'd introduced you to a new, talented author, Kara Galloway. Her first title, Temptation #322, *Sleight of Heart*, was a spoof on the paranormal.

As we already know from reader mail, the alliance of romance and the supernatural is a popular one. In *Love at Second Sight*, Kara has surpassed herself. Her intimate knowledge of paranormal phenomena, combined with her powerful sense of drama, makes *Love at Second Sight* a riveting tale of cosmic dimensions. Follow Charlie's mind, travel through time and space and, like Ross, you'll find yourself spellbound....

Because *Love at Second Sight* is so different, we've chosen to highlight it for you and make it an Editor's Choice. As usual, we're eager to hear your comments on this selection. Happy reading!

The Editors
Harlequin Temptation
225 Duncan Mill Road
Don Mills, Ontario, Canada
M3B 3K9

Love at Second Sight

KARA GALLOWAY

Harlequin Books

TORONTO • NEW YORK • LONDON
AMSTERDAM • PARIS • SYDNEY • HAMBURG
STOCKHOLM • ATHENS • TOKYO • MILAN

Thank you, Norm, for everything

Published May 1991

ISBN 0-373-25447-4

LOVE AT SECOND SIGHT

1

"WE'LL BE LANDING at Stapleton International Airport in approximately ten minutes," the captain announced in a relaxed drawl. "Temperature down there is a balmy seventy-six."

Charlie Yost adjusted her seat back into its upright position before the patrolling flight attendant could find fault. Chicago to Denver flight 103 tipped and, through her window, Charlie had a view of the late-afternoon sun slipping behind a white barricade of mountains and clouds. Somewhere in that awesome line of stone and snow, there was a job to do and five days in which to do it—solve the what and the where of the Sayers tiara.

AT GATE B21, Ross Davies sprawled in an orange plastic seat, doing one of his least favorite things—waiting. He squirmed, leaned forward, arms on knees and stared at the carpet below his clasped hands. Then he sighed and fished his sister's telegram from his shirt pocket. It read:

BE AT STAPLETON SAT MAY 20 CONTINEN-TAL 103 TO MEET CHARLIE YOST. HAPPY BIRTHDAY. MANDY.

One birthday Mandy had given him a brown, refrig-erator-sized carton full of white foam pellets in which were buried two tickets to a Who concert. Another year it was a fruit basket with one bite taken out of every apple. Last year the stack of Western paperbacks she sent him was bundled together by means of an elastic athletic supporter.

Ross sighed again and tapped the telegram back into his pocket. Whoever this Charlie Yost birthday present was, he wasn't someone Ross looked forward to meeting.

A plump hand extended a can of pop across his shoulder. Ross took it and nodded his thanks. The row of seats jiggled when Evan James collapsed into one of them. Ross wasn't sure why his graduate assistant had insisted on coming along to the airport; Evan obviously hated waiting, too. He'd visited the rest room, the gift shop and three vending machines, all within fifteen minutes.

Now Evan jabbed his glasses higher with a middle finger to the nosepiece and intoned, "So what do you think, Ross? What's this Charlie Whatshisface going to do for you? Measure you for a suit? Teach you Russian? Clear up zits?"

Ross, whose only complexion problem for the last fifteen years had been how to shave whiskers out of the cleft in his square chin, popped open the drink and swallowed half of it without pausing for breath, thereby earning the rapt attention of a toddler across the aisle.

"Say, wasn't Charlie Yost that guy *Time* wrote up a couple weeks ago?" Evan said. "Mafia informer looking for a safe house?"

The first passengers walked out of gate B21. Ross stood up as the arrival lounge filled rapidly with people greeting people. "How the hell do I know which one is Charlie?"

Evan drained the last of his Sprite and burped appreciatively. "Look for scars on the face, dark glasses, pinstriped suit, violin case."

A blur of blue caught Ross's eye, and his expression smoothed into pleasure as he focused on the woman moving away from the congestion. She stood by the windows scanning faces.

Backlit, the demure, long-sleeved azure shirtwaist became a siren's gown, outlining slender arms, softly rounded breasts and hips, and hinting at the origin of those long, long legs. Even her feet, in sensible tan T-straps, were shapely.

Ross blinked, realizing he was staring. He glanced at her face with its aura of golden hair, and found her staring at him.

Evan, having spotted her, too, muttered, "Forget Charlie. Let's pick up Charlene."

Then she started walking toward them, stopping beside Ross, smiling at him tentatively.

She reached across her chest to adjust the strap of her shoulder bag. "Ross Davies?"

Fighting an unexpected urge to shout "Hallelujah!" he held his smile in the polite range as he said, "Charlie Yost, I bet."

Charlie had located Ross the moment she emerged from the arrival tunnel, but shyness had made her step aside to muster up her confidence before approaching Mandy's brother. He looked just like his photograph. She hadn't thought of him as handsome till she saw the tall, tanned body under that lean, clear-eyed face.

Awkwardly, she pushed her hand forward, and his strong fingers clasped it in quick acknowledgment.

"You know my sister well?"

"Well enough to guess she didn't mention Charlie was a female."

"A most pleasant surprise." He allowed the smile to grow.

Evan cleared his throat noisily; Ross stepped back to bring him into the conversation. "Charlie, this is Evan James, my graduate assistant. You know I teach American history at Colorado University?"

"Yes. I understand you're accepting another position at Berkeley in the fall. Mandy—" Charlie's voice disappeared under the blare of the public address system calling Mr. Benevita to a white courtesy phone.

"Let's find your baggage and a quieter place to talk," Ross decided, touching her elbow. "Been to Colorado before?" he asked as they walked along the glassed hallway toward the main terminal.

Charlie waved one hand toward the panorama. "No. This boggles the mind. And you get to see it every day."

"Till he throws it over for California," Evan remarked. "Course California's got some great scenery, too, if you don't mind it rearranging itself every few years." He made appropriate sound effects with his mouth.

"I take it you aren't crazy about Ross leaving?" Charlie tossed a quick smile over her shoulder at Evan's expressionless face.

"Naw, I can hardly wait," Evan said. "He's going to leave me his Mr. Magoo bottle opener and Farrah Fawcett poster."

Ross ignored them, peering at the ceiling computer screens to determine which carousel would spew forth Charlie's luggage. He led her to the rim of the as yet unmoving conveyer.

Glancing back at Evan waiting on the fringe of the crowd, Ross said, "He's a great kidder."

"It's okay. I'm used to being teased, myself." She turned to grin at him and caught him studying her face. Unembarrassed, she studied him back. *Nice blue eyes*, they both thought, and then the baggage conveyer squealed into life, breaking the spell.

The first two suitcases to tumble out of the chute were Charlie's. Then they had to wait nearly five minutes for the third, cosmetics, case to make an appearance. They talked about Chicago versus Colorado winds while surreptitiously trying to identify each other's after-shave and perfume.

"Shoes?" Ross asked, hefting the cosmetics case onto the floor.

"Books." She let Evan have the one case she was carrying, and they hiked out to the parking garage.

"Glad we're parked on the top level, halfway back," Ross said. "I didn't have time for the rowing machine this morning."

"I'm sorry those are so heavy. Maybe I could stand here with my baggage while you go get the car?"

"I was just teasing," Ross assured her. "There's an elevator."

Their steps echoed in the open concrete building. Traffic forced them into single file, and Charlie, behind Ross, admired his broad shoulders straining against the weight of her suitcases.

"Mandy Davies is a reporter on the *Sun Times*," Evan remarked offhandedly once they were in the elevator.

Charlie nodded and laughed. "Is this a test?"

"I just wondered if you work there, too."

"No. I'm one of you. I teach at Chicago State University."

They looked at her expectantly. "Psychology," she added.

"Curiouser and curiouser," Evan said.

The door shuddered open and they trooped toward a battered white van with tinted windows all around, a CU parking lot sticker in one of them. As Ross unlocked the rear door, Evan grasped Charlie's arm and drew her firmly aside.

"Don't get too close, ma'am. You've heard of Fibber McGee?"

"That's just it," Ross agreed, peering inside before swinging the door wide open. "My very own mobile closet. You name it, it's in here, or you don't really need it."

Charlie ventured forward and inventoried the nearest items—skis, snowshoes, canteen, bicycle pump, tripod, tool chest, rope, four stacked wastebaskets, a bag of potato chips.

"Did you trap that gorilla that was living in here?" Evan asked. "You'll never be able to jam Charlie's luggage in there. I'll help—I'll eat the potato chips."

Ross pushed and piled and finally made room for the luggage.

"Okay, com'ere, Charlie, you're next," Evan joked.

"I think I'd prefer to ride up front," she said. "Or is it just as bad?"

"I forget," Ross said, shaking his key ring and ushering her into the front passenger seat.

Except for a road map of Wyoming, a gum wrapper and an airport parking ticket, the seat was empty. Scrambling into the row behind, Evan studied the Sprite can he'd forgotten to trash, and, with an elaborate shrug, tossed it backward over his shoulder.

"Hey," Ross snapped. "You'll break something."

They paid at the exit booth and rolled into Denver traffic. Charlie pretended to watch the air traffic congestion on her right—one plane after another, all sizes, alighting and scooting out of the path of the next. But she was really thinking about getting Ross alone and telling him the reason she'd come. It occurred to her he would have probably welcomed the information before they left the airport; it might have saved him the trouble of driving her straight back to it.

"So how's a foxy lady like you get a name like Charlie?" Evan asked, offering the potato chip bag over the back seat.

"No, thanks." She shifted sideways. "My mother was frightened by an Yvonne DeCarlo movie. The name is Charlotta. I could hardly wait till I could talk so I could order everyone to call me Charlie."

"Why didn't you just go by your middle name like all the rest of us who hate our first?"

She turned to look him in the eye. "Bobette?"

Everyone laughed. Ross's delighted chuckle gave her a pang, reminding her of her father.

"Charlie's definitely better than Bob," he said. "Besides giving you an outlandish name, did your parents mistreat you in other ways?"

"Actually, I had a very happy childhood. My dad managed the municipal swimming pool, and Mother had a homemade candy business. I was one of the most popular kids in town."

"Where was this?"

"Southern Indiana. Which looks a bit different from Colorado." She leaned to look through Ross's side window but found herself examining his profile superimposed against the Rockies, the sharp lines of his nose and jaw softened by unruly blond hair spilling over his forehead.

"It's amazing," she blurted, feeling like a smitten schoolgirl, "how flat the land is coming in from the east, and then, wham, a wall of mountains. It must have intimidated the pioneers."

"Not for long. Once they discovered those speed bumps had golden linings," Evan observed, "good old greed populated Colorado."

"Negative," Ross said. "The go-backers were the greedy ones. They went back East when anticipated fortunes literally didn't pan out. The people who stayed became farmers, ranchers, merchants, whatever, and a few of them did strike it rich."

"What did they strike besides gold?" Charlie asked, thinking about her mission.

"Silver, copper, lead, tungsten—"

"Ski resorts," came from the back seat. "Coors beer."

Ross triggered the headlights. Traffic, which had been fierce, began to thin as Denver disappeared behind the van.

"Hey, Ross," Evan demanded. "When you going to give Charlie the pop quiz on why she's here?"

"When she's ready, she'll reveal all."

Ross's choice of words startled Charlie. She cast him a sharp look, but he was concentrating on passing a dump truck, his shadowed face blandly innocent.

"It's a little involved. I'd really rather wait till Ross can give me his full attention," she answered Evan. His brash personality was beginning to irritate her, like sand inside a shoe.

Ross adjusted the rearview mirror an infinitesimal degree. "How's Mandy? What's my hotshot sister doing these days?"

"Still covering city affairs. Government. She won a regional press award for a story she did about substandard housing. Doesn't she write to you?"

"I think she felt as if she were throwing her letters down a sewer when she wrote to me. I mean, I'm not very good about answering back. I do call her now and then. I'm sure she never mentioned you."

Evan's imitation of Peter Lorre was barely recognizable as he said, "Say, how do we know Mandy did, in fact, send that telegram? Say, maybe the real Charlie Yost was dressed in a bunny suit, carrying a big bouquet of balloons. Charlotta, who won the '86 World Series?"

"Ignore him," Ross said.

"Mandy and I met when she wrote a human interest article about me for a Sunday supplement. We hit if off right away, and, one thing leading to another, we're sharing an apartment now."

Ross spared her a surprised glance. "She moved?"

"She didn't. Your mother did. I hope you knew your mother would be in Europe for the summer? I'm keeping her room warm for her until I find something more permanent."

"So what did this news article say about you, Charlie?" Evan asked.

He kicked the back of her seat, rearranging his legs, and Charlie was suddenly aware of a growing headache—a line of pain behind one eye.

As she remained silent, he probed further. "What makes you so special?"

"Nothing," she answered, wondering how she was going to disclose her psychic abilities to Ross.

AT THE FIRST RED LIGHT in Boulder, Ross asked Charlie where she was staying.

"Mandy said—I thought Mandy made arrangements. With your aunt." She groaned and dropped her forehead into her fist. "But I bet she didn't. That rat!"

Ross's mouth twisted against a laugh. "Aunt Esther's gone to rendezvous with my mother in France. I'm baby-sitting her house. There's plenty of room, but there's no chaperon."

"Sounds ideal to me," Evan piped up. "Your sister sure knows how to pick presents."

As Ross automatically obeyed the green light pointing him left, Evan said, "Hey. Don't forget Brenda."

"Oh, yeah, I did forget, too." Ross ducked his head to check the outside mirror before making a two-lane change. "Apologies, Charlie. I have to stop and see someone a minute."

The van wound up into streets full of university buildings, old trees and young pedestrians. The latter, in T-shirts, shorts and carrying backpacks, streamed in all directions, unintimidated by the traffic.

"Hasn't the spring term ended?" Charlie asked.

"Next week is finals."

They slipped out of the congestion into a narrow side street bordered by Victorian houses perched on steep little lawns. Ross drew the van to the curb at the only available spot, next to a fire hydrant.

"Be right back," he promised, bumping the car door open with a shoulder and leaping out.

Charlie watched him stride across the street and up concrete steps to a miniature porch bright with red geraniums. Ross rapped at the screen door. A slender woman materialized and pushed the door open. Ross yanked it open wider and disappeared inside.

Evan unbuckled his seat belt. "Come on, Charlie, everybody out."

"Out? Why?"

"He thinks he's here to pick up some insurance papers Brenda wants his advice on. It was my job to be sure to get him here. Because it's really a surprise party." Evan hauled open her door and helped her negotiate the step from van to curb.

"Who's Brenda?" she asked, reluctantly following Evan across the street.

"She's a professor at the university, too. Old friend. Hurry up, we'll miss the best part."

Charlie hoped Ross liked his surprise better than she did. She'd been looking forward to a bathroom, a drink of cold water, bare feet. She wasn't a party person, especially when the entire guest list was composed of strangers.

Hustling her onto the porch, Evan opened the door without knocking and ushered her into a dim hallway that smelled like tomatoes cooking. Forefinger to his lips, he tiptoed forward.

Out of sight somewhere ahead, Brenda, presumably, was laughing. "Did she pop out of a cake?"

Ross started to say, "Mandy's got more imagination than—" and an explosion of voices brayed, "Surprise!" Laughter was the next explosion. All need for quiet gone, Evan marched Charlie down the remainder of the hallway to the kitchen.

Ross stood near the center of the small room with its cluttered counters, Brenda's slim arm around his waist. They faced an archway into a dining room where a dozen grinning faces were clearly enjoying Ross's confusion and their own sneakiness.

Evan brushed his fist across Ross's forearm in a good-old-boy gesture. Ross threw Charlie a rueful look. Then his friends engulfed him, handed him a goblet and swept him into the adjoining room, everyone talking and laughing.

Brenda swiveled gracefully and extended her hand to Charlie. "I'm Brenda Gates." She had dark eyes, a cap of red-blond hair and a dimple in one cheek.

"Charlie Yost," she answered, shaking Brenda's cool, dry hand. "I feel like a gate-crasher," she admitted, raising her voice over an outburst of hoots and catcalls.

"Oh, no, please. Make yourself at home. We're all easy to get along with." Brenda's hostess smile faltered as something smashed in the crowd.

"It's okay, Bren," a male voice yelled. "My mom will knit you a new one."

Ross announced, "My closet's parked by a hydrant. I'm going to move it."

He strode into the little kitchen. Nearly colliding with Charlie, he closed strong, steadying fingers on her forearms. Behind him a lanky, dark-haired man said, "Here, Ross. I'll move your van," and Ross released her to dredge up the key. The man winked at Charlie and trudged toward the front door.

"Brenda, this is Charlie Yost," Ross said, putting a hand on each woman's back. "She's a friend of Mandy's."

"We're way ahead of you," Brenda informed him. "We're already at the point where I ask her if she wants to freshen up before she runs the gauntlet in there."

"That would be wonderful," said Charlie.

"I'll show her where," Ross said, lightly increasing the pressure on her back. When they were in the hall alone, he bent to mutter in her ear, "I'm sorry about this, Charlie. If you want, I can get Evan to run you home."

"I'm fine if no one objects to my staying."

"Uh, do you want to give me a hint about why you came to Colorado? So I can tell my friends?"

"What you said to Brenda was just fine. I'm a friend of your sister." She certainly didn't want to try to explain

Mandy's plan in these few seconds before the guests came to reclaim him.

The lavatory was a tiny, slant-ceilinged room tucked under the second-floor stairs. As the door snapped shut, she glimpsed Ross returning to the kitchen, rippling tension out of his shoulders and smoothing his hair.

In the gilt-framed mirror, Charlie smoothed her own hair and made token adjustments to her makeup for as long as she decently could.

SHE PAUSED SHYLY at the threshold of the yellow-and-white striped dining room. Ross stood alone beside a trestle table stacked with colorful packages, the well-wishers sitting in a circle of high-backed chairs arranged along the walls.

Arms folded, he teetered on his heels and glanced from face to face. A sheen of perspiration highlighted his hairline. Grimacing, he threw up his hands. "I didn't realize you all hated me this much," he said to the ceiling.

While the laughter flared, Charlie stepped sideways into the room and slid down cross-legged on the blue braided rug. In the chair closest to Ross, a young woman with ebony hair hanging straight to her waist turned to bare her braces in an unself-conscious smile.

"Hurry up and open something before it begins to smell," someone down the line urged.

"Let the unwrapping begin."

"Take it off, take if all off," a girl encouraged, shimmying suggestively.

Ross raised both hands for quiet, which only instigated some people to shout "Speech!" Shaking his head in frustration, he crooked a finger into the argyle-patterned paper of the first gift on top of the pile; it turned out to be an old Van Halen T-shirt with the sleeves torn out.

Ross held it to his chest and fluttered the ragged edges. "Did the last owner survive the attack?"

"Sorry, Ross, my cat helped me wrap it."

"It's the latest look, Ross. Nouveau busted."

"Gee, Peg, you could have at least washed it before you wrapped it."

All the presents were like this one—gags, and after each was opened, the repartee ricocheted around the crowded room. Charlie rested against the wall, enjoying the jokes, saying nothing herself, watching Ross. At one point he glanced in her direction and did a double take, studying her gravely; it was as if for a moment he'd forgotten who she was. Then someone swayed into his line of vision, demanding his attention.

Shortly after that, Brenda announced the "nitty-gritty"—food. There was a polite stampede to the kitchen, where pizza and nachos and an overflowing platter of raw fruits and vegetables were laid out buffet style.

Charlie hesitated, hunger deferring to shyness, till Ross threaded his way to her, a full plate in each hand, and offered her one. "What do you drink? There's coffee, tea, cola."

"Thanks. I'll just go with this for now. I hate to balance my meals."

He rolled his eyes. "Another comedian."

He steered her to a chair beside the tall, serious-faced man who'd volunteered to move the van. "Charlie, Paul McCoy here is my office mate. He teaches American history almost as expertly as I do. Paul, Charlie Yost."

"Ah, yes, the mysterious birthday bestowal," he said, but quietly and with none of Evan's mocking inflection. "Hi, Charlie."

Almost everyone else was in the kitchen or standing in the archway. Before Ross could sit down, he was called.

"Com'ere so we can take your picture with Brenda and the cake."

Charlie watched him stroll toward the summons before he was swallowed up by the crowd. Between shoulders, she saw him plant a kiss on Brenda's forehead. As Brenda hooked an elbow up behind his neck, someone stepped into Charlie's view. Whatever happened next, it made the spectators cheer.

"Hope you don't mind it too much."

Charlie turned, startled, to face Paul.

"Being party to a party," he elaborated.

"At least nobody's trying to sell me plastic cookware." She smiled around a forkful of refried beans.

Ross came back, wiping his mouth with a napkin. The noise level quieted to the clinking of spoons in cups and the crackle of corn chips and celery being chewed. Into the calm, a male voice called from the front hallway. "Hey, Ross, is that your van up the block? Someone just broke the back window."

Ross leaped up and was gone. Plates and cups were slammed down, and the party drained outside. Brenda looked in at Paul and Charlie, shrugged, then followed the stragglers into the street.

Paul continued to eat, but Charlie, remembering her suitcases, stood up. "Save my place."

"I doubt if anyone will want to sit on your mozzarella," Paul said, transferring Charlie's plate from her hand to her chair.

"Excuse me," she said, pushing her way through knots of people standing on the front steps.

Paul had found a parking place a few doors farther up the block. Although the street was dark now, a light from one solitary lamppost illuminated the rear of the van. Charlie recognized Ross's straight back as he and four buddies approached the van, walking rapidly but warily. When they were within feet of the back door, it burst open, cascading boxes. Another door slammed and feet pounded. One spidery figure, running hard, evaporated into shadows half a block away.

Ross and his friends milled around, examining the damage.

"What was going down?"

"Looks like he got away by kicking that stuff on top of you and hightailing it out the front."

"That sucker could run. We need him on the track team."

"Did he get anything?"

"See if my Sprite can's still in there," Evan shouted.

Charlie gently elbowed her way to the place where Ross's belongings and her suitcases littered the street. Light gleaming in his hair, Ross bent to lift things into the van. Two men scrambled to help. As one of them grabbed the handle of the cosmetics case and swung it upward, the lid sprang wide, avalanching books.

"Darn, no underwear?" Evan asked before stooping to help Charlie retrieve her things. He reversed a handful of books to read the spines. "What is this anyway? *Science and the Supernatural . . . Challenge of Psychical Research. . .*" He scrabbled on the pavement and brought up more titles. "*Mind-Reach . . . Channeling.* For crying out loud, Ross. Your pretty little birthday present is a goddamn witch!"

She wanted to slap Evan. Instead she rescued her books from him, stuffing them every which way into the case to get them out of sight. Of course that meant the lid wouldn't shut. Fighting a mixture of anger and apprehension, Charlie began fiercely rearranging. Over her head, people were discussing her.

"What do you mean, 'present'?"

"You mean what does he mean, 'witch'?"

Ross's face dipped in front of hers as he leaned over to help. He wasn't smiling, but he wasn't frowning, either. Unable to think of anything witty to say, she remained miserably silent. Putting a knee on the case to snap the catch, he rose and tossed it into the van, as if it weighed nothing.

Brenda was picking up shards of glass from the street, holding them flat on one hand. Ross touched her arm, scolding her and saying he'd take care of it. They straggled back to the house where everyone resumed places and retrieved plates, and the party continued at a more subdued level. Paul, working on a second helping, lifted Charlie's plate from her chair to indicate "welcome back."

The ebony-haired girl sat down on the other side of Paul and peered past him to ask, "So, are you psychic?"

Paul, having missed the action on the street, snorted into his coffee cup.

Evan dropped into the chair on Charlie's right. "If she was psychic, she'd have known someone had broken into the van."

Brenda strolled up. "I'm sorry, Charlie. In all the excitement, I haven't introduced you to anyone. This is Mary Spring, Charlie Yost." Brenda waved her hand in the appropriate directions and then stepped back to make a general announcement that Charlie was a friend of

Ross's sister, visiting from Chicago, and everyone should introduce themselves before the evening was over.

As the crowd acknowledged this in a polite babble, Evan's smug voice took up the cudgel again. "So is she a medium or what?"

She had wanted to break it to Ross gently. Mandy had warned her that it would be difficult to convince Ross that Charlie was as committed to and capable in her field as he was in his. Here in this good-time atmosphere, where everything was a joke, she'd have no chance to explain her mission or to do so with dignity.

But faces turned toward her, eyebrows up, mouths curved expectantly, and Evan, at her elbow, prodded her along the plank with, "Wanta feel any bumps on my head? Or anywhere else?"

"My field is parapsychology. I chose it because I seem to have some ability for retrocognition—seeing the past. I've found lost children and pinpointed spots to dig for water and helped solve a murder. I don't predict horse races or bend spoons. As for why I came to Colorado— I'm here to vacation in your beautiful Rocky Mountains." She spread her hands and looked questioningly around the room.

Her eyes locked with Ross's as he lounged, arms folded, in the doorway. His face was still expressionless. Damn, but he looked good.

The thought made her grin, and he glanced down at himself as if to check that everything was in order. That made her grin more expansively, and she tore her eyes away before he'd begin to think she was simpleminded.

"How fascinating," Mary Spring proclaimed. "Tell us about the murder."

To Charlie's relief, Brenda swept into the room just then bearing the flaming cake. While the "Happy Birthday" song swelled exuberantly, Ross extinguished the candles by fanning them with a napkin amid groans and protests.

The revelry went on into the night. Brenda's semifinished basement became a dance floor, with music furnished by a rock and roll radio station. Those who preferred, as Charlie did, to sip wine cooler and talk, stayed in the relatively quiet dining room, sprawled on the floor, using friends as backrests. Charlie sat on one chair, her shoeless feet propped up. Every half hour or so, Ross or Paul would go outside to check on the van.

Once Evan pulled a chair up to the trestle table and stretched his arms along the top in either direction. "Let's hold a seance." But no one seconded the notion.

Though everyone was politely friendly, Charlie felt herself very much the outsider, especially since Ross seemed to be, deliberately or not, constantly occupied elsewhere. By midnight she longed for the party to end. Mouth stiff from smiling, eyes gritty, she fought down an outbreak of yawns. In the midst of a contest to see who could hold a note the longest without taking a breath, someone announced, "I gotta go," and suddenly everyone was leaving.

The hallway rang with good-nights and thumping feet. The house hushed. There was the rustle of wrapping paper being deposited in a wastebasket, the snick of Brenda's lighter to a cigarette, the tap-tap of ice dropping from the automatic maker. To allow Ross to thank Brenda in private, Charlie stepped onto the porch and found Paul sitting on the top step.

"My esteemed colleague says I may ride home with you. My home, I mean," he said, holding out his hand to be helped up. "Too tired to ride my skateboard."

She chuckled at the mental image of Paul's scarecrow figure atop a careering skateboard.

As they strolled toward the van, she nodded at the ruined window. "What was that about, do you think?"

"Some tough wanting something to hock or fence. Don't folks do that in Chicago?"

"I'm trying to recall," she laughed softly.

Paul tested the side doors—locked—and came back to prop a foot on the bumper. "We can get in through the rear, but that's only if we're masochists. Let's wait for Ross."

She swiveled to look up the street. "Where's Evan?"

"Hitched a ride home with a carload of women. He's not as dumb as he acts."

"He's certainly skilled with a needle."

"Right, well, he's a good kid. Emphasis on 'kid.' He's the classic, ultraintelligent but not too attractive boy who grows up admiring himself since no one else will do it for him. He's a history ace, so he's a big help to Ross."

Brenda's screen door slapped. Ross finally came striding up the street. He smacked the side of the van as he passed, like a cowboy caressing his horse. Without comment he unlocked the doors, let Charlie climb in unaided and hauled himself into the driver's bucket to shudder the van awake.

The sidewalks and streets were deserted now, except for the occasional tavern patron or homeward-bound Romeo. They dropped Paul in a cul-de-sac of apartment houses. He gave Charlie's shoulder a friendly pat on the way out. As Ross swooped the van around the circle, Charlie stretched her legs and tipped her head back. The broken window wheezed.

"Now," Ross said, "what's all this buffalo chips about you being psychic?"

2

IT WOULDN'T HAVE stung more if he had slapped her. "I beg your pardon?" she said in a tone as cold as ice.

"I want to know right now if my sister paid your way out here, and what she thinks she's getting for her money." A stop sign gave him an excuse to vent some anger on the brake.

"Ross, it's one in the morning, three o'clock Chicago time. Can't we discuss this after a few hours' sleep?"

"What is there to discuss? What's so difficult about answering some questions? Did Mandy pay you, yes or no?"

"No!" She glared through the windshield. "Not yet."

"But you've got some kind of verbal agreement. Can you give it to me in twenty-five words or less?"

The grade of the road was gradually steepening, and Ross downshifted. To their right, the city was a blanket of lights.

"Mandy knows my past successes at finding things psychically. She thought it would be fun to try it on locating the legendary family treasure."

"Oh, brother!" He shook his head.

Charlie's headache was back—bang—like a thrown switch. "If I determine what and where the Sayers tiara is, Mandy will pay my airfare and expenses. If I don't, she'll still pay half."

"And did my frivolous sister happen to mention that the so-called tiara is probably up in the Rocky Mountains on land we Sayerses no longer own?"

"Yes. She just wants to—"

"She's spending good U.S. dollars for a swami-ette to produce a treasure that none of us could keep anyway?"

"Mandy *said* you'd be pigheaded."

Ross gave the steering wheel a vicious wrench, and they jerked to a stop in front of a double garage. He leaped out, stamped around to the the garage door and shoved it so hard it was still rocking when he berthed the van beside a blue sedan. Amidst much grunting and banging, he hauled Charlie's bags to the floor and wrestled them into the house.

Carrying only her purse, Charlie yawned behind one hand and waited numbly to be shown her room. The pain in her eye blurred her vision—it threw a yellow aura around Ross's head. When he led her down a back hallway, he seemed to be glowing like some avenging angel.

It was a nice house, not large or new, but thick with carpeting, plush furniture and bric-a-brac. He ushered her into a white-and-gold room with a brass four-poster and an adjoining bath. This was obviously the master bedroom.

"Aren't you using this room yourself?" she asked.

"No. I'm in the spare room." He thumped the baggage down.

"Aren't you afraid I'll steal the candlesticks or the dresser set?" Wanting to collapse onto the bed, she squared her shoulders and stiffened her back, instead.

The gesture wasn't lost on Ross, who'd raised his eyes just then to the mirrored closet door. Momentarily bemused by Charlie's graceful profile, he saw her breasts lift and felt his fingers twitch involuntarily.

"Arrgh," he said and escaped the room, poking his head back inside for a moment to announce, "Tomorrow, let's blame this whole bad idea on Mandy, shake hands and go our separate ways."

The last thing he saw, as he reached to yank the door shut after him, were her startled eyes—glazed with fatigue, Colorado sky blue, boring straight into his sensibilities.

As he got ready for bed, he analyzed his reaction to Charlie. He wasn't really as angry as he'd pretended, though it certainly irritated him that two women assumed they could manipulate him. The notion of clairvoyance would be laughable except for Charlie's obvious faith in it. Talking with her would be like dealing with a religious zealot—embarrassing and boring and a prodigal misuse of his time.

He lay back, hands clasped behind his head, and stared at the ceiling. What bothered him most was that this eminently desirable woman handicapped herself by believing this garbage. He sat up and pounded his pillow before stretching to switch off the lamp. Pigheaded, huh? Better than air for brains.

CHARLIE WOKE in the temporary confusion of a strange bed. The fat, brass-cased clock on the nightstand said nine o'clock. Sitting up slowly in deference to her lingering headache, she rested her head on her updrawn knees and as she did every morning, tried to recall her dreams.

A scene involving Ross's lean face flirted at the edges of her consciousness. Something pleasant. From experience she knew to relax and wait. But this time nothing more materialized, and she threw off the covers and stood up.

Flexing neck and back, she walked to the window to examine the view, a disappointingly small slice of lackluster backyard. Somewhere in the house a door chunked open or shut. She hurried to unearth a favorite man-tailored shirt and denim skirt and some silky lingerie that it always seemed a shame to hide under her clothes. Making up in the little white-and-chrome bathroom, she felt like a matador preparing for the arena.

"Ho, toro," she muttered, opening the door and following the scent of coffee down the hall.

She found the kitchen with its spectacular view. Her host, spectacular in his own sexy way hunched over the Sunday funnies at the dinette table in a floor-to-ceiling bay window overlooking the city of Boulder. The morning sun glistened in his hair and glowed on his skin. Dressed in jeans and a bright red undershirt, he looked more like a student than a professor.

Her step on the threshold made him turn and peer gravely over half-frame reading spectacles. She gave him her most dazzling smile.

"What a delightful lookout." Self-consciously she strolled into the room. "Is there more coffee?"

He thumbed backward over his shoulder. Charlie found a cup after trying three different cupboard doors.

As she poured the black, fragrant liquid, Ross cleared his throat. "How come you couldn't guess which door was the cups?"

"Is that a real question, or are you just baiting me?" She joined him at the table, smiling another, softer smile.

He took off his glasses. "I guess I was baiting, but on second thought, it's a real question."

"Psychics aren't superpersons with X-ray vision. It usually takes some mental preparation to receive information using extrasensory perception."

"You mean ESP requires you to go into a trance."

"No." She sipped at the tongue-numbing coffee. "I mean that ESP is not a parlor trick I can perform on cue. It's not like a fisherman dragging in a fish; it's like being very still and letting the fish just swim in."

"So if I quit talking and you concentrate, you could tell me where we keep the gravy ladle?"

"The only way I can hope to convince you of my ability is to demonstrate it. Do you have time for that now?"

He made a show of consulting his watch. "How many hours would it take?"

"Isn't twenty-four the traditional deadline?"

He didn't smile. His austerity made Charlie feel like a freshman having an audience with a dean.

She sighed. "Did you ever play heavy-heavy-hangs-over-thy-head?"

He did smile then, a nasty, condescending smirk.

She looked away, out the window, and continued, "There's a standard psychometric experiment that's a version of that old game. Instead of guessing what's being held over her head, the psychic gets information by touching an object."

"You want me to hand you an item, and you'll tell me its history. Is that the idea?"

She turned toward Ross and caught him studying her face. "Yes, that's it."

Ross knocked back the last of his coffee and stood to pour another cup. "I'm not saying that if you pass this test I have to let you try to find the alleged family treasure."

"Of course not. This isn't a bet. It's simply a demonstration."

He returned, frowning, to his chair. After a thoughtful silence, he asked, "Something wrong with your hand?"

"No. If you massage the base of your thumb, here, it relieves headache."

"Want some aspirin?"

She laughed. "Ross, why would I need aspirin if I have my thumbs?"

He regarded her with the interest of a naturalist who'd come upon a new, exotic species. "I'll bet a week with you would be the most fascinating, exasperating time of my life."

"And I'm sure I'd find you equally exasperating," she answered. Relenting, she added, "And fascinating."

Ross gave himself a mental shake. "Okay. So we need an object."

"Don't give me anything that belongs to Mandy or Evan or anyone I've met. You'd claim afterward I was using information I already had, instead of channeling off the object."

Ross pushed up from the table and left the room. A minute later he returned, right palm extended toward Charlie. On it was a rock about the size of an Eisenhower dollar and a couple inches thick, its color a pale gray that caught the light and glittered silver.

As the stone changed hands, Ross felt the warm brush of her fingers, and there was a snap of static electricity, a common phenomenon in dry climates, but one he'd never particularly enjoyed before. He expected her to examine the rock; she scarcely glanced at it, enclosing it in one slim fist. Changing position to stare at the sky, she took several exaggerated breaths. Ross quietly settled into his chair, rested his folded arms on the table and waited.

In less than a minute, Charlie began, "Rows of bodies. Or people in line. Not people. Animals. All kinds of animals. A zoo? They're near a wall, maybe a barn. They don't move. They just seem to be waiting for something."

It wasn't Ross's notion of a trance. He felt certain he could pinch her and she'd react with instant indignation. Her clear eyes seemed fixed on a scene that her soft voice described in the manner of a person speaking to a blind friend.

But nothing that she'd said so far had anything to do with the object he'd given her.

She began to speak again. "A woman with long hair arranged in a knot on the nape of her neck. She's very pale. White. And fat. Huge. She's staring at something." Long pause. "I think she may be dead."

Ross's face, too, was frozen and expressionless when Charlie turned to him. She glanced at the rock before handing it over.

He played with it, rolling it in his fingers, oddly disappointed to have been proven right. "Sorry, kid, no cigar."

Her troubled eyes sharpened with surprise.

"That part about the hair in a knot might be my grandmother," Ross said, "except she was a tiny thing and one-fourth Arapaho, definitely not fat and not white." He held the rock higher between forefinger and thumb. "This was my grandfather's whetstone. He used to whittle, mostly toys for his children—soldiers and dolls. Come on, I'll show you."

Leading Charlie to a glass-fronted corner cabinet in the living room and opening both doors wide, Ross stepped aside with a wave at the display of wooden carvings.

"Ohh," she breathed. "Aren't they wonderful!"

All of the unpainted figures were less than five inches high. Most were men—cowboys, Indians, soldiers, miners. Each was different; even the soldiers held distinctive poses. The largest figure, a baby with the misshapen head and flat features of a newborn, was swaddled in a scrap of much-washed quilting.

Charlie touched the material with a respectful fingertip. "This is a treasure right here. Your grandfather was very gifted."

Ross lifted out a drummer boy and held it near his face. "Any resemblance? They say this was my uncle."

"Maybe," she conceded. "It was your maternal grandfather? Are any of these carvings of your mother?"

He grinned. "That infant you've fallen in love with."

She grinned, too, then bent to study the rows of carvings more closely. "No animals."

Ross's smile faded as he briskly returned the drummer to his shelf. "A dog or a cat, maybe. Uh—yeah, there."

"But what I saw in my vision was a regular Noah's Ark."

"Yes, well, I guess you dialed a wrong number."

Charlie backed away to sit on the overstuffed arm of a massive sofa. "And you don't know a very fat, very pale lady?"

"No, thank goodness."

She looked so forlorn, Ross had a sudden, almost brotherly, urge to put comforting arms around her, which led him to an interesting speculation on how her body would feel pressed against his. Suddenly she pinned him with a look so forbidding he was afraid she'd read his mind.

But then she said, "I'm not making excuses for what is apparently a failure on my part, but it's an established fact that skepticism can interfere with psychic capability."

"Oh?" He folded his arms and waited politely.

"When there's a hostile observer, his negative thoughts can block the psychic's efforts."

"I see. If you fail, it's my fault. If you don't fail, it's in spite of me. And now you want to try again for the best two out of three falls?"

"No, I want my second cup of coffee," she said serenely, preceding him into the hall.

Her perfume beckoned. This time the feeling it stirred in him was definitely not brotherly.

Lounging in the doorway, watching her as she carried her cup to the table, Ross asked, "Want some toast with that?"

"Nope, thanks." She shifted to face the window again. "Are those pink buildings part of the university?"

He came to stand behind her chair, the better to enjoy the smell of her perfume. "Right. The red-tiled roofs. The one shaped like a mine is engineering. That skyscraper off by itself is a dorm."

On the horizon a yellow glider, looking as fragile as a toy made of balsa wood and airplane glue, spiraled gracefully.

"Charlie, don't feel bad about the treasure. It probably doesn't even exist. According to a journal Grandma Sayers kept, it was 'Timothy's,' my grandfather's. That's all any of us know about it. She only mentioned the treasure once near the very end of the book, when she wrote that 'they'—we don't know who—'buried Timothy's treasure today.' She didn't use calendar dates, but we think the entry was made in the summer of 1909. The family has done some halfhearted exploring of the mountain homestead, but generally we regard it face-tiously as the 'Sayers tiara.'"

"None of the children—your aunts and uncles—re-membered hearing any discussion of a treasure when they were small?"

"There were six kids. The two oldest were boys who died in their teens in a mining accident. The oldest girl was a year old and the other three weren't born yet in 1909. No, they didn't see or hear stories about a trea-sure."

"Do you have the journal?"

"It's in with the carvings. But looking at it would be no help. It's mostly a record of births and deaths and when crops were planted and how deep the snow got. Nothing as exciting as Grandfather striking gold."

"But if I could hold the book for a moment—" She twisted around to appeal to him.

"Charlie," he scolded softly, watching the sensuous curve of her mouth. "You had your chance, and I wasn't impressed."

Her fist hitting the table made him start. "I don't un-derstand," she exclaimed. "It felt right. The images were very strong. You aren't telling me I failed just to get me out of your hair, are you?"

He circled to his side of the table to sit down before answering with clipped civility. "Dr. Yost, I assure you, I wouldn't lie just to support a theory."

"It isn't 'doctor.' Yet. And I apologize." She bumped the table, standing up, rattling china. "I guess I'd better find a motel and rent a car and get on with my vacation."

Ross jumped up, too, sending the table top into in-stant replay. "You don't have to move to a motel. Mandy would never forgive me."

"I don't want to intrude on your life any further."

"No, no. In fact, I'd like to show you some of the territory myself." Now that being rid of her was a distinct possibility, Ross was perversely reluctant to let her go. "We could picnic in the mountains, for starters."

"Don't you have exams to prepare?"

"All done. Tomorrow and Tuesday the poor souls have to fill them in, and then I've got a week for grading. Evan does a lot of it."

"Well," she said, drawing out the word, making up her mind. "I've always loved picnics."

"Great. You finish your coffee and I'll make the lunch."

While he spread mayonnaise on bread, Charlie watched, amused that he could be this charming now that the threat of her psychic powers had been, in his opinion, neutralized.

"What would you usually be doing today?" she asked.

"Hiking the high country. Looking for ghost towns and old mines."

"Alone?" She thought of Brenda.

"Sometimes Evan goes along. He's helping me research an article right now. Victorian architecture above ten thousand feet."

"Could you do that today? I mean, it sounds interesting. I'd like to go with you."

He speared a cherry tomato with the tip of his paring knife and popped it into his mouth. "Two things. Have you got comfortable walking shoes?"

She nodded. "Tennis shoes."

"Not the best, but they'll do. And how's your blood pressure? High altitude can make a flatlander sick."

"Do the symptoms include headache?" she guessed ruefully.

"That and shortness of breath. Dizziness."

"Almost like being in love."

He stopped sawing at the baked ham and contemplated the ceiling. "Yes, except for the coughing and limping and nosebleeds."

"High altitude causes all that?"

"No—I meant when I fall in love."

She laughed, and he attacked the ham with renewed vigor.

After changing into jeans, Charlie found Ross in the cool garage boarding over the broken window. "Did you ever do an inventory to determine if the thief got away with anything?"

"It looks like all he got was practice and exercise."

She surveyed the interior of the van. "Maybe it would have been a blessing if he'd taken some of this stuff off your hands."

"Bite your tongue! Every item is a gem that might come in handy some day." He reached to pull out a bullhorn, flicked it on and thundered, "Vote for me." Charlie covered her ears. "What do you need a bullhorn for?" she demanded

"Pep rallies. Parades." He patted it as he pushed it behind the passenger seat. "Actually I thought it was a mobile phone. Till I had trouble picking up incoming calls."

He liked her laugh—a low, genuinely happy sound.

They drove up Flagstaff Mountain, where the road switchbacked steeply and a wrong twist of the steering wheel would launch them into free-fall, with plenty of time to not enjoy the ride. Coming to a fenced area labeled Boulder Mountain Park, they bumped across the dirt road and stopped at the shoulder to admire the view. Cloudless blue sky melted into the earth's gray-green curvature.

Charlie jumped out to take pictures she knew would never convey the grandeur since she didn't have a wide-angle lens. As she turned she found Ross studying her; flustered, she glanced around the parking lot. "Is this where we picnic?"

"Not unless you're starving. There's a more private, romantic place I have in mind." He ignored her arched eyebrow.

The road up from Boulder continued on into mountains behind Flagstaff. It narrowed, turned to rusty dirt, and roller-coastered constantly, with a rocky creek tumbling in tandem. Dark evergreens. Red stone walls. In the side ditches, wildflowers—white, yellow and purple.

"Now are you starving?" Ross asked after almost an hour.

"I'm so hungry I could eat a ham sandwich."

The road was about to bank right between natural gateposts of free-form rock. Instead Ross steered straight across a shallow ditch, up a gentle slope, dry bushes slapping at the undercarriage. The grade leveled off and deteriorated into a dry wash cobbled with boulders.

"Everybody out. Carry something," Ross commanded.

Charlie wrapped the camera strap around her neck, hefted the thermos, let him drape a blue plaid blanket over her arm and hopped out. The cool air prompted her to pick up her sweater. A breeze off some nearby glacier puffed her hair into her eyes as she watched Ross shoulder the pack containing their lunch.

He gestured like a wagon master and marched off. She followed, concentrating on the uneven footing, enjoying the exercise after a morning of inactivity. The path was uphill.

"Where are we?" she asked Ross's back.

"This is Roosevelt National Forest land, almost Rocky Mountain National Park. Pretty soon we'll meet up with a stream called Choke Creek."

"Any snakes up here?" she asked, using a flat, warm rock for a handhold through a nest of boulders.

"Too cool. They're at lower elevations." He turned his head enough to flash a smile at her. "Like Boulder."

When it seemed they'd reached the crest, the land dipped for twenty feet and then rose again. Choke Creek gurgled on their left now, a clear trickle of melted snow.

Charlie found, to her shame, that her breathing had grown labored and loud. If Ross noticed, he pretended not to, though he offered twice to stop for rest, and the second time she agreed. They lounged against a mammoth slab of rock that warmed their backs while the sun warmed their faces. A hawk wheeled high overhead.

"Look at this," Ross said, dipping two fingers into the creek to bring up a pebble. It gleamed gold and rose and soft white on his palm.

"Nature's jewelry," Charlie said.

"But watch when it dries."

As sun and breeze licked up the moisture, the stone's colors faded to a uniform, drab tan.

Ross stared glumly at his hand. "Ever since I was a kid, I couldn't understand that." He flipped the pebble back into the water. "There's a moral in it somewhere."

He squared his shoulders and squinted at the path ahead. "About a block farther on is a boulder shaped like a whale. You can walk up its tail and sit on its head and contemplate the cosmos or your chocolate bar or whatever. Are you with me?"

"Why do I feel like a donkey following a carrot?" She sighed, gamely shoving away from the supportive rock.

Ross put a strong hand under her elbow to haul her forward, let the hand slide down around hers, and they climbed for another few minutes.

The whale boulder jutted out into the creek. Crossing the tail gangplank, they spread the blanket on the smooth body and dangled their feet over the brow. A yard below their soles, the creek danced to its own music.

As they ate, Charlie complimented the chef on a superb meal.

"The ambiance ain't bad, either," he said, lying back to absorb the sun.

Finishing her sandwich, Charlie rolled over on her stomach beside him. Contentment made her smile into the crook of her arm. Then some itinerant devil jabbed her with jealousy as she wondered how often Brenda had reclined on this same rock. She was tempted to try a reading and see.

"Tell me about you, Charlie. Ever been married?"

"No, not even close. Fellas always fall into two categories. They believe I'm psychic and they're nervous that I'm reading their minds, or else they don't believe I'm psychic and think I'm a space case."

Ross picked a leaf out of her hair so deftly she didn't know he'd moved. "I don't think I fit into either of those groups."

"What then? You think I'm not psychic, just a charlatan?"

"I think you're a sensitive, intelligent woman who's been badly misled by educators that she innocently trusted."

Her arm muffled her giggle. "Do you know how pompous you sound?"

"When did you decide you had ESP?"

"Fairly late in life. Not till college. I got interested in what you'd call occult stuff—dowsing, clairvoyance, out-of-body experiences—and I tried some of the exercises and tests the experts outlined, and it appeared that what I could do was channel off objects to describe the past. Psychometry."

"You said you'd found lost children."

"That's nice." She raised her head to smile at him.

"Sorry?"

"Usually it's the murder case people ask about first." She rolled onto her side and propped her head on one hand, facing him. "I helped a detective friend on a couple of runaways. But the best thing I ever did was read a toddler's teddy bear. We found the boy in an open field just before a blizzard. He's fine." She tipped her chin in an unconsciously defiant gesture.

"What do you do? I mean, what happens to you when you—what was it—*read* an object?"

"It's a form of self-hypnosis. I've learned to quickly, completely relax and blank out the physical world. Then I tell my subconscious what it is I want to know. And then it's like flying. I split in two, and half of me is up above looking down at whatever scene unfolds. It's exhilarating."

"It sounds scary."

"It isn't frightening unless the scene I'm tuning in on is frightening. Like the murder." Her voice roughened. "A wife batterer. He got tired of bruising his knuckles and took a hammer to her."

Ross winced mentally. "Aren't you afraid to let yourself go like that? What if you can't get back to the real world?"

"There are tricks of the trade. When you begin meditating you imagine your left foot, for example, anchored to the ground. And when you want to come home, you remember the foot, the link to reality. To keep in touch with their bodies, some psychics picture a ray of light."

Ross did a graceful pull-up and sat, elbows on bent knees, staring at the churning creek. "I'm sorry, Charlie. I just can't fathom it. There's no scientific explanation—"

"But they're working on one. There are lots of theories."

She pushed forward beside him, earnestly resting her arm on his back as she pleaded her case. He felt a delicious burning through his shirt.

"That's why I brought all those books," she was saying. "To show you that some extremely intelligent scientists are investigating some very good possibilities that—" She faltered to a stop as Ross twisted around and kissed her.

3

HER EYES WIDENED before they slowly, gladly, closed. After the sweet, gentle touch of lips to lips, they swayed away from each other, considered, and tried it again. Ross shifted to put his other arm around her, his hand reaching to explore the liquid texture of her hair. Her fingers tightened against his back, curled into a fist and then unfolded to knead the knotted muscle.

Still, it was a tender kiss. Charlie felt as if her mouth was melting under the warm, soft pressure of his. Deep inside her pelvis, desire uncoiled.

The tip of Ross's tongue lightly stroked her lower lip, and then, touching her forehead with his before drawing away, he said, "You taste good."

"Likewise." The casual response didn't betray the pounding of her heart.

Ross was as surprised as Charlie by the unpremeditated kiss. The proximity of her cool cheek and warm mouth tempted him to sample again. He yearned to scoop her into his lap and see where rougher kisses would take them.

Resolutely he jammed his hands into his jacket pockets and glanced around. "We better pack up."

"Okay." She felt a quick flash of disappointment and mentally scolded herself as she scrambled up. Mandy hadn't sent Charlie to Colorado to romance her brother!

Whey they bent to lift and shake out the blanket, the errant thermos fell over and rolled into the creek.

"I'll get it," Charlie said, running down the whale's tail and jumping to the weedy bank.

The vacuum bottle had floated several yards downstream before nosing into a rock-pile barrier near the edge. To avoid getting her feet wet, Charlie knelt as close to the water as possible and braced one hand on the shallow bottom, stretching to retrieve the thermos with the other.

"Yow, that water's cold!" she complained.

Ross finished folding the blanket and turned to check her progress. Still crouched with a hand in the creek, Charlie was clutching the thermos to her chest, eyes blank and wide. Following the direction of her gaze, Ross saw nothing but the usual bushes, dirt and rocks.

"What's wrong?" he called, and when she didn't answer, he leaped down the boulder to put a palm on her bowed back. "Charlie? You okay?"

"She's here," Charlie said, her submerged fingers ghostly in the clear creek.

"You'll freeze your hand," he chided softly. "Who's here?"

She stood up slowly, staring at the water beaded on her hand. "The pale woman."

"Come on, Charlie, I thought we agreed—"

"I saw her again. Plainly. When I touched the water." Narrowing her eyes, she sighted up the creek bed. "This place has something to do with your grandfather." She turned to fix him with an accusing glare. "Is the cabin near here?"

Ross kicked a shower of gravel into the creek. "It's up the canyon a ways."

"I want to see."

"It's too far. It'd be dark before we could get down again."

"Then say you'll bring me back another day."

"I don't want to promise that. You're on a fool's errand, Charlie."

"Fool, huh?" She shoved the thermos at him and wiped her hands on the legs of her jeans. "That's exactly why I want to come back. To show you I know what I'm doing."

Ross stamped to the boulder to grab up their belongings.

"What are you so stubborn for?" Charlie demanded. "What have you got to lose if you humor me? Huh? If I find the treasure, terrific. If I don't find it, what have you lost except a few hours in which you could have been watching TV or something?"

"I don't want to encourage you, Charlie. I can't sanction this paranormal nonsense." He pushed the blanket and her camera into her midsection. "Let's move out."

Following him down the trail was much easier than their trek up had been. "Albert Einstein believed there was something to it," she shouted at his back. "Sigmund Freud. Edison. Churchill. Madame Curie. Ouch!" This last was a result of Ross's suddenly stopping and Charlie's bumping into him.

He turned around, lower lip protruding. "It's my treasure. If I don't want to find it, you've got no say."

"It's Mandy's, too," she reminded him. "She's the one who hired me. In fact, now that I know the Sayers homestead is up this canyon, I don't need you. I can come here without you and work in peace!"

"Oh, no, you don't." He grabbed the front of her sweater and pulled her close to him. "It's dangerous to hike up here alone. What if you fell and broke a leg or got hit by lightning or ran into a bear? You aren't coming up here without me."

Her belligerent mouth slowly slid into a smile. "Thank you. You won't be sorry," she whispered.

He considered swearing. He wanted to shake her. Instead he brushed his mouth across hers in the barest of kisses. Nudging her chin up with his nose, he fitted his lips into the hollow of her throat.

Beside his left ear, her voice murmured, "Edgar Mitchell, the astronaut."

"What?" he wondered, distracted by the feel of her pulse beat against his cheek.

"He believes in ESP."

"Oh. Well," Ross said, hugging her to him before swinging around to resume the hike. "You should have told me about him in the first place."

By the time they reached the van, the sun had fallen below the mountains. It felt good to slip into comfortable seats and close the doors against the whining wind.

Charlie sorted through a stack of maps she'd noticed earlier wedged under her seat. Spreading a Boulder County geological survey map over her lap, she watched alertly through the windshield, on the lookout for road signs.

"Don't trust me, huh?" Ross remarked.

"I just like to know where I am. Should anyone ask."

He glanced away from the road three times, scanning the map, then jabbed a finger into it.

She marked the spot with her own finger, and studied it for a moment. "Oh, right, here's Choke Creek."

"I'm tied up tomorrow. How about if we make it an overnight camping trip Tuesday and Wednesday?"

"That would be a very nice," she said, as if she'd just accepted a cup of tea at a garden party.

They drove home by a different route, no less scenic than the first. After several miles, satiated by beautiful vistas and suffering from a bout of jet lag, Charlie cushioned her head against the side window with her rolled-up sweater and fell asleep.

Ross poked Vivaldi into the tape deck and tapped the steering wheel in time with the stately beat, not really listening to the music. He was planning out the rest of his week with Charlie.

NO SOONER had they driven into the garage than Paul strolled up the driveway, bearing pizza and a six-pack of beer. A car door slammed down the street, and Brenda jogged up to overtake and pass Paul. She did it beautifully in spite of her high heels and tight skirt.

"Hey, we thought you might need rescuing from Ross or vice versa," she told Charlie. "We brought supper."

The four of them made short work of the pizza, sitting at the kitchen window with the lights of Boulder glowing below. Charlie had been sitting quietly, sipping beer, enjoying the lively conversation flying among the other three until Ross noticed she was drowsing in her chair and sent her to bed.

She took a quick shower, the hot water wonderful against her skin. Toppling into bed nude, she squirmed with pleasure between the crisp, cool sheets and fell asleep to the sound of Brenda's laugh.

WHEN CHARLIE WOKE, the brass clock pointed at eleven o'clock, and light seeping around the curtains indicated it was morning. Wrapped in a terry robe, she opened the hall door to listen to the silence of an empty house.

"Ross?" she called, sure he'd gone to work hours earlier.

He'd left a note, still attached to a yellow legal pad, propped against the coffee canister. It read:

Gone to interrogate. Be back at noon to take you to lunch. Don't look for the journal because I took it with me.

R.

Impossible man, she thought. *I wouldn't have snooped like that. Besides, I didn't get up soon enough.*

Ready early, she did admire, once again, Grandfather Sayers's carvings, studying each tiny face through the glass, her hands behind her back. When the inner garage door slammed, she went to welcome Ross. Each entered the hallway from opposite ends and stopped, eyeing each other.

"Good morning. Afternoon," she corrected, thinking, *I've kissed that sexy mouth.* The memory sent an arc of pleasure through her stomach.

"I thought we'd have lunch on Pearl Street, if that suits you." His hands jingled change in the pockets of his cord trousers.

"Fine. What's Pearl Street?"

Pearl Street was in downtown Boulder; it was a pedestrian mall built in the sixties. The first thing Charlie admired, when they'd parked and walked a block, were the flowers, mostly brilliant geraniums and jewel-colored petunias, hanging from lampposts and spilling out of ground planters on the brick paving. At a corner, Charlie stopped to admire a bronze statue—a young woman on a porch swing, the motion of her hair and skirt frozen by the sculptor's hand.

Office buildings of soaring glass and stone. Retail shops of every architectural persuasion. Assorted restaurants—Greek, Italian, Irish—some with outside tables along the promenade. Ross touched Charlie's elbow to guide her to one of these.

"Sun or shade?" he asked.

"What happened to smoking or nonsmoking?"

She slipped off the jacket of her navy poplin suit to take full advantage of having chosen to sit in the sun. A young man in safari clothes brought menus and ice water and disappeared again for so long Charlie changed her mind three times about what to order.

When the waiter finally returned, she asked for quiche, Ross ordered a fresh fruit platter, and they settled back to wait. Just outside the railing next to Charlie's foot, a pigeon bobbed in an erratic path. The faint strum of a guitar being tuned drifted down the block.

The parade of people, dressed in everything from pioneer to punk, fascinated Charlie: a scrub-faced woman in a long dress and hiking boots whose German shepherd wore a red neckerchief; a young Goliath dressed in camouflage coveralls with a red rose boutonniere; a clown leading an imprecise formation of preschoolers singing "Small World"; a toddler in a squeaky stroller, his mouth stretched to completely enclose a sucker. Charlie turned to point out this last to Ross and found him, once more, staring at her.

"Sorry," he said, picking up his water glass for a diversionary drink. "You're very attractive."

"I've thought the same about you." She liked the way the open collar of his white dress shirt framed his tan throat.

"You ought to get some hiking boots." He looked off into the crowd and added, "That is, if you're still determined to go up to the homestead."

"Wouldn't new boots be worse than old tennis shoes?"

"Not if you have an expert fit them. And socks. Heavy socks. Tennis shoes are too light. You'd feel every pebble."

"All right. Is there somewhere along here to buy boots? And do we have enough time before you go back to work?"

"Yes and yes. We'll also need a new thermos. I forgot to look at the old one, but it rattles since its escape attempt."

A half block away the guitar began a country song and was joined by a nasal female voice. Charlie glanced around at the two hirsute musicians in jeans and T-shirts, guitar case open at their feet inviting contributions.

"Do I need a backpack?" she asked.

"I've got extras. I also have a sleeping bag you can use."

A flippant remark came to Charlie's mind, but she didn't feel secure enough to say it.

Their food arrived, fresh and inviting. Ross gave Charlie a sample kiwi fruit as she had never tasted any before. She devoured everything on her own plate as if she'd missed several meals.

Once they'd finished lunch, they walked the length of the mall. On the county courthouse lawn, people sat or reclined like living statues. Charlie waved aside Ross's offer of dessert—cotton candy from a street vendor. She shook her head at the man who wanted to photograph her beside a life-size cardboard Lee Iacocca, only two dollars. Ross put a companionable arm around her waist as they paused to watch a troupe of youths tumbling on narrow mats laid out on the brick path.

"Is it always this lively?" Charlie asked, moving on slowly, hoping not to dislodge Ross's casual embrace.

"Saturday nights are even livelier. And on Halloween there are thirty thousand people jammed into these four blocks." He shifted his hand to the small of her back, to steer her across an intersection. "Let's try Banana Republic for your boots."

She let the clerk and Ross tell her what she wanted, but she hated the unwieldy high-top leather boots they put on her.

"Frankenstein's bride," she observed, laughing at the contrast between her footwear and her classic suit. "Ross, I don't think I could walk from here to the van in these, let alone hike up a mountain."

The clerk brought out khaki canvas lace-ups he called French Foreign Legion boots. "If you spray these with water repellent, they're almost as good as leather for keeping your feet dry. Unless, of course, you get caught in a flash flood."

On the way to the checkout, Charlie tried on a great-white-hunter type fedora, saw that Ross was sincere when he pronounced it perfect, and added it to her boots and wool socks purchases. Consulting Ross's watch, they struck out more purposefully toward the parking lot.

"If you want to wrestle this around awhile," Ross said, jerking his thumb at the van, "you can drop me off and take it for the afternoon."

Honored that he would trust her with his favorite saddle horse, Charlie asked shyly, "Could I come with you?"

"To the university? What is this, a busman's holiday?"

"I'd like to do some reading at the library. Acquaint myself with this area."

"Oh?" He glanced, unseeing, at the keys in his hand. "What exactly do you have in mind? You going to check if any circus trains carrying animals and a sideshow fat lady ever broke down in these parts?"

"Good suggestion. But I was thinking more along the lines of general geography, history, whatever else would make me more knowledgeable and less tenderfooted."

"Okay." He shut her in and skirted the front of the van. "Okay," he repeated, hopping into the driver's seat. "But you can hang out in my office. Between the two of us, Paul and I have all the Colorado texts fit to print and some that shouldn't have been."

The campus streets teemed with young men and women wearing the preoccupied expression of students undergoing the rigors of exams. Ross homed in on a macadam parking lot tucked behind a multistory, rose-colored brick building. At the double-door entrance, he and Charlie were engulfed by a dozen exiting students, a few greeting him with "Hi, Dr. Davies."

The cool hallway exuded the universal schoolhouse scent of chalk, paper and people. Far off, a metal door clanged. Their shoes echoing on the hard tiles, Ross and Charlie passed a hushed classroom of students taking a test, climbed one flight of eggshell-patterned stairs, and turned down a side hall to an oak door with brass lettering: Am. Hist. In smaller letters it said: Dr. Theo Paul McCoy and Dr. Ross S. Davies. Using his key with the effortless motion of long practice, Ross waved Charlie inside.

It was, on first impression, a small room with three tall windows overlooking evergreen trees. On further consideration, Charlie saw it was really a generously proportioned room made small by the furniture and books that had been crammed into it.

Ross lifted a stack of books from the seat of a visitor's chair, twisted in search of a place to put them, redeposited them on the chair and said, "You can use my desk."

"The one with the Mr. Magoo bottle opener attached to the side."

"Correction. The desk that's attached to the Mr. Magoo bottle opener."

"Of course. Forgive my faulty perception."

He used his hands like snowplows on the desk top. "Help yourself to whatever you want to read. All these bookshelves are mine. Those are Paul's, and he won't mind if you browse through his." Glancing at his wristwatch, he grimaced, stirred the desk surface to find the necessary exam papers and left her.

Charlie balanced her purse atop the papers Ross hadn't taken and draped her jacket over the back of his oak swivel chair. Cocking her head at the spines of the books, she drew out a fat text titled *Colorado Ghost Towns* and used it as a base for a "to read" pile that soon became precariously high.

Settled into the squeaky chair, feet tucked under her, she was miles away in Leadville's ice palace, when she was startled by a single rap on the door preceding Evan's clumping into the office. A smaller, dark companion trailed him like a shadow.

Evan stopped short, threw a protective arm in front of his face and declaimed dramatically, "The witch! 'Speak then to me, who neither beg nor fear your favors nor your hate.'" Regaining his composure, he ambled over to the desk. "How you doin', mama?"

The other young man hovered in the doorway, and Evan didn't encourage him with an introduction.

Charlie, ignoring him, too, tried a friendly but impersonal tack. "Did you know there was a five-acre castle built in Leadville in 1896, with a stairway, two ballrooms, a dining room, and a skating rink, all made of ice? Five thousand tons of ice!"

"Oh, sure. I remember it well. Beautiful. But the heating bill was outrageous. Ross around?"

She laughed at Evan's deadpan humor before answering his question. "Giving an exam."

Even put his hands on the arms of Charlie's chair and rolled her backward. He smelled as if he'd overdosed on the Old Spice. "S'cuse me, ma'am. I just need some stuff out of this drawer."

She pretended to return to her reading.

"So did you talk Ross into giving you a shot at uncovering his treasure?" Evan leered at her over his shoulder to emphasize the double entendre.

To avoid saying something equally rude, Charlie stood up, stretching, to examine the view out the nearest window.

"I sure wish I had some mysterious fortune requiring your attention," Evan said, opening and shutting drawers. "Overnight, in the middle of nowhere. Mmm-mm! Sure would be nice."

Although Charlie certainly didn't appreciate this, Evan's friend snickered. Ashamed that they could embarrass her, she pretended she needed a break. As she passed the lurking doorkeeper, he bared his teeth at her and whispered, "I'm Cid," as if it were classified information.

She scouted out a rest room and made minor cosmetic repairs without benefit of makeup, as she'd left her purse behind in her rush. When enough time had elapsed for Evan to collect what he needed and leave, Charlie went back to the office. Paul's much thinner outline now leaned over Ross's desk.

He glanced up and smiled welcomingly. "I thought you might be in the vicinity. Ross doesn't usually carry a purse to work. I was writing him a note, but maybe you'd pass along the message."

"Sure."

"Brenda wants him to pick her up at seven-thirty."

Charlie struggled to keep smiling. "That's it?"

"Ross will understand." Paul moved to his own desk and picked up a battered briefcase.

"What does Brenda teach? I don't recall anyone saying." Charlie's voice conveyed polite interest.

"She's in civics, U.S. government. And that lady is brilliant, believe you me. She'd be the perfect first female president."

"Maybe I'd better get her autograph, just in case." Charlie laughed to dilute the underlying sarcasm.

Paul trudged toward the door. "You know a psychic wouldn't be a bad idea for president, either. Be a boon to our foreign policy."

Charlie slumped into Ross's chair and lifted the next book from the stack. "Right."

"What a political ticket the two of you would make. Bright Brenda for logic and charming Charlie for creativity. See you."

She stared glumly at the closing door. "Brenda for brains," she explained to the empty room. "Charlie for kooky notions."

Impulsively she swung her feet onto the top of the desk, ankles crossed, skirt bunched above her knees. Okay, admit it, she scolded herself. You're jealous. No right to be. But no question, jealous.

She opened *Rocky Mountain Travels*, began to read, and after a page or two, comprehended, as well. Absorbed by the drama of David Moffat's railroad tunneling six and two-tenths miles through solid rock at the Continental Divide, she didn't hear Ross come in.

Absorbed in his own academic thoughts, Ross had momentarily forgotten that Charlie would be waiting for him. His heart jolted at the sudden sight of her, sunlight haloing her hair, one slim hand poised to turn a page and her magnificent legs stretched to meet his desk. Like an inexperienced schoolboy, he gawked, letting his fingers relax enough to spill exam papers over his shoes.

Charlie, startled like an ambushed deer, slammed her feet to the floor and sat forward primly, smoothing the skirt over her knees, watching Ross retrieve what he'd dropped.

"I had a high school science teacher who graded tests like this," he said, "only on a stairway. The papers that fell on the top step got As and the next step got Bs and on down." He straightened, his face rosy with embarrassment. "At least that's what he claimed."

"I wasn't expecting you yet. Do you want your desk?"

"No, just hand me that attaché case. I'll take these home to work on."

"Doesn't Evan do that for you?"

"These are essays I'll need to grade myself. He's doing a couple other classes whose papers were multiple choice. Did he come by to get the test keys?" Ross pulled open the left-hand drawer. "Looks like they're gone."

"He was here. And Paul was here and said to tell you that Brenda wants you to pick her up at seven-thirty." Charlie brushed miniscule lint from the hem of her skirt.

"Ach! I forgot. There's a faculty meeting tonight. Drat."

Charlie smiled. Only a faculty meeting. "Do you mind if I take some of these books home to read? I'm a pretty fast reader, but there's so much fascinating material, I'd like to study it in more detail."

"No problem. We've got a shopping bag around here someplace. Here it is. Let's fill it up."

He held it open by the handles while she stuffed in books. She smelled like fresh air and freshly cut grass, and he imagined he could feel her body heat radiating out to lap his skin. The weight of the bag bunched his arm muscles; the rest of his body tension was Charlie's doing.

She glanced up from depositing the last book, and something in his expression held her eyes. He stood rooted, arms aching. Then he slowly lowered the bag to the floor and eased the pain by drawing Charlie into an embrace.

"I can't seem to keep my hands to myself," he whispered against her temple.

They leaned into each other, her head tucked under his chin, savoring the tender, undemanding moment. Then he slanted his face to reach her mouth for an equally tender, undemanding kiss. For several minutes, nothing existed except their two bodies fitted together like pieces of a puzzle, making a whole.

Charlie sighed pleasure and regret as Ross reluctantly eased his mouth away from here. On the outside, she was very still; deep inside, she writhed.

"Maybe this overnight camp-out isn't a good idea," Ross said abruptly.

She frowned.

"I mean, maybe you'd like a chaperon."

She stepped away from him, amused. "And maybe it's you who needs the chaperon. I'm not afraid of you, Dr. Davies." She playfully tweaked his nose.

He trapped her hand and kissed the palm. "You're right. I'm the one who needs protection."

To his surprise, Ross realized it was true. Charlie did scare the hell out of him. But he would need some time to figure out why.

THEY PICKED UP fried chicken and fixings at a drive-in on the way home and shared a companionable supper in the kitchen, watching the Boulder sky fade toward evening.

Ross sat up straighter and looked at his watch. "Gotta go! The faculty meeting starts in ten minutes. Oh-oh, what did I do with the agenda?" He leaned to rummage through his attaché case on the floor by his chair. "Okay, where is it?" he demanded in a suddenly cold voice.

Bewildered by the question and his obvious anger, Charlie asked, "Where's what? The agenda?"

"No, damn it. The *diary*.. My grandmother's journal." He stalked to get the book bag and dumped it across the table.

"Ross, I haven't seen it. Where did you have it last?"

"Don't give me that mother-knows-best routine. It was in my attaché case at my office—as you must have discovered." He gave up sorting through the pile of books to fold his arms across his chest and glower. "Why the hell did you have to sneak it out behind my back? I'd have shown it to you. Sometime."

Standing, she mirrored his stance and expression. "Ross, I did not touch the journal."

"Well, no one else would have. You're the only one who's been dying to see it."

With ominous restraint, she asked, "You want to pat me down?"

In a different mood, he'd have come up with a witty reply. This time he whirled away, throwing up his hands.

"Maybe you took it out of the briefcase at your office," she suggested, slam-dunking paper plates into the trash can. "It's probably somewhere in your desk."

"I'll check. In which drawer do you advise me to look?" he sniped.

Charlie's scowl should have singed Ross's hair. He charged out of the room, into the garage and van, and punished gears and brakes on his trip down the driveway. She swatted the refrigerator with her fist, swal-

lowed hard and went to sit at the table. It was several
minutes before she'd calmed down enough to pick up the
first book and lose herself in Colorado history.

As before, the incredible mountains and stubborn
people who populated them held Charlie in thrall. Pages
flew with the time until, roused by the sound of the big
garage door, she straightened her posture and looking at
her watch realized that three hours had passed.

She devoutly hoped Ross had found the journal.

From the ring of his heels on the concrete floor, she
guessed he had not. She jumped up to draw a glass of
water and turned her back, anxious to avoid facing him.

"Hello," he said in a distant, professorial way.

"Hi. Good meeting?" She turned around and lounged
against the counter, sipping the water.

"I didn't find the journal." He loosened his tie and ran
his hand through his hair, leaving strands at endearing,
odd angles.

"I didn't take it," she said softly. "It hurts that you think
I did."

"Let's just forget it. It'll turn up someday." He walked
to the table and thumped the attaché case onto a chair.

"Ross, I wish—" She braced herself for his rejection.
"I want to get a reading from your briefcase, see if I can
determine the whereabouts of the journal."

His mouth twisted into a mirthless grin. "You're going
to prove you're a psychic by, quote, *finding,* unquote, the
journal? Come on, Charlie, I wasn't born yesterday."

She blinked against the sudden sting of tears. Setting
the glass down blindly, she murmured, "Good night,
then," and fled.

When he heard the door of her bedroom click shut,
Ross rubbed his eyes wearily and walked down the hallway to his own room. While he undressed and show-

ered, he ruminated on Charlie's ability to, first, scare him and, now, disappoint him. Obviously he was strongly attracted to her, which was alarming to a thirty-six-year-old bachelor. And now that she'd done something as petty as take his journal and then lie about having done so, he was, naturally, disillusioned about her character.

That's okay, he told himself, punching out his pillow and stabbing at the lamp switch. Chicago's a long commute from Boulder, and even farther from Berkeley. Save yourself for all those California girls.

Thirty feet away, Charlie lay in the dark, her eyes open, admonishing herself for caring this much about the opinions of a man she'd known only two and a half days. *Caring* was the word, all right. She could, she was sure, care very much for Ross Davies. She flounced from her left to right side, rolled onto her stomach, sat up to arrange the blanket, snapped on the bedside light, hitched the pillow into a backrest, and, jaw clenched, began to read about Colorado's Indians. One chapter led to another.

Abruptly her whole body twitched and the book thudded shut, rousing her from her concentration as, from the depths of the house, a clock chimed midnight.

Otherwise the house was still. Charlie pictured Ross's attaché case sitting on the kitchen chair, waiting to tell her what she wanted to know.

She slid out of bed and wrapped the terry robe around her bare body. She went barefoot to the hall door, cracked it enough to determine the coast was clear, and with ghostly stealth, glided to the kitchen.

Moonlight whitewashed the room and all its contents. Walking over to the attaché case, Charlie put the tip of a tentative index finger against it, then knelt beside the chair, carefully laid the case down on the seat and tested the latches. Not locked, they flew apart—snick, snick.

Without opening the case, Charlie kept her hands on the twin latches, her fingers lightly exploring them, as if she were reading braille. Breathing deeply, closing her ears to the persistent drip of the nearby faucet, Charlie lifted her face toward the window and waited.

She felt herself beginning to float, the kitchen dropping away. The moonlight brightened to garish yellow and the outline of another room began to form below her like an aerial view of a roofless building. Peering down at the human shape in the center, she focused and zoomed—a living camera—and the scene sharpened on hands holding a battered, brown-paged book.

Without warning, the light exploded and Charlie plummeted to the floor.

"Now what are you doing?" Ross filled the doorway. His burgundy robe, hastily wrapped around him, hung crooked; his hand dropped away from the light switch and dangled at his side, clenching and unclenching.

"Evan has the journal," Charlie said dully, not yet free of the vision. She'd sat down hard, legs outstretched. Spontaneously she tugged the robe across her legs.

"Evan has the journal?" Ross walked across the room and stopped just short of stepping on her. "Evan has the journal."

Nodding, she resisted the impulse to scoot backward, away from his looming stance.

Ross squatted, his face inches from hers. "Which one of you had the idea? It sounds like the sort of dumb prank Evan would pull, but since the point is to convince me that you are, no kidding, psychic, maybe *you* thought it up. Huh. You really thought I was that gullible?"

Charlie flinched as his hand reached toward her, but it grasped her shoulder gently. "Ross, I'd like to go to bed now."

"Is that an invitation?" He caressed her upper arm while his eyes glittered dangerously.

"No. Just leave me alone, please."

He spoke so softly, she could scarcely understand the words. "Charlie, Charlie. Why couldn't you be an ordinary woman?"

"Why don't you call Evan and ask him why he took the journal?" she whispered in return.

Ross shook his head in baffled exasperation. The fire gradually cooled in his eyes, and he took both Charlie's hands to pull her to her feet.

"I'll walk you to your door," he said softly.

4

CHARLIE PRECEDED ROSS into the hallway, numb with defeat. "We didn't discuss what time we'd leave in the morning," she said.

They stopped at her door and Ross subjected her to a critical, searching look. From the moment he'd left his bed to investigate the furtive rustlings in the kitchen, he'd throbbed with suppressed excitement. His anger with Charlie was fed by the anger he felt toward himself, for the weakness that had clutched his stomach muscles at the sight of her sprawled on the kitchen floor. She had looked so vulnerable with her wild hair and frightened eyes, the disarrayed robe tantalizing with flashes of breast and thigh. He'd raved at her because he wanted to protect her. And himself.

But the barrier of rage had burned itself out; his body smoldered with nothing but desire.

"Charlie," he began, "I'd really like to sleep with you tonight."

He leaned to kiss her, only his mouth touching her, all his experience and skill and enthusiasm focusing there.

But she didn't kiss him back.

When, discouraged, he relinquished her velvety mouth and leaned away to see her impassive eyes, she said, "Have you changed your mind about going tomorrow? Or does it depend on whether I sleep with you tonight?"

"Of course not!" he protested, a sinking sensation in his stomach. "I'm not an extortionist."

"And I'm not a thief or a liar or a charlatan." She hit his chest with a small, frustrated fist.

"I believe you, Charlie," he said, surprised that he really did. He tried a cautious smile.

"Oh, sure." She rubbed her cold arms and scowled at him. "Tonight you'd tell me anything you thought I wanted to hear."

"I'm sorry!" Ross spread out his hands in a gesture of self-righteous innocence. "I haven't had much experience seducing women, and I'm botching it up something awful."

"Well, now you know how I feel, being accused of something I had nothing to do with."

"Let's start all over," Ross pleaded. "I should have answered you when you first asked, 'We'll leave for the homestead at nine in the morning.' Even though it's probably a wild-goose chase."

Encouraged by the promise of a smile flirting on the corners of her mouth, he continued. "Now that the topic of the hike has been taken care of, we can talk about the weather, sports, inconsequential, nonthreatening topics till we're both mellow again."

He straightened, wiped his hands on his robe, and gingerly wrapped them around her arms. "Next I slowly make tactile contact, like this. And then I bring you closer, like this. And then I kiss you. Like—"

This time her mouth was welcoming. It invited him to stay, to taste, to drink, to devour. He braced himself against the doorjamb, weak-kneed, the fire in his groin a delicious, relentless ache. His right hand laced into her hair. His left hand fumbled for the doorknob.

Charlie wrenched her face away from his. "No," she sighed.

He let go of the knob and trailed the knuckles of that hand along her chin, down her throat, into the cleavage of the terry robe. She stopped him, her hand over his.

"No. I'm not teasing. I'm very—attracted to you. But we can't make love tonight without ruining the rest of our time together."

"I don't want to hear this." He kissed her eyelids, the tip of her nose, tried to fasten his mouth over hers.

She twisted out of his embrace. "If we're intimate to-night," Charlie faltered, "tomorrow you'll feel guilty and I'll feel embarrassed, and nothing will be easy between us anymore."

"Why should there be guilt and embarrassment if we're two twentieth century consenting adults?" he argued.

"Do you love me? Do I love you? How do you know I won't get pregnant? Do we ever expect to see each other again? Should either of us put aside lifelong values for a half hour's sexual gratification?"

"Oh, God! This lady's a psychologist all right."

"Come on, Ross," she said, stepping completely out of his grasp. "I'm better than a one-night stand, and so are you."

He shoved his fists into his robe pockets to restrain himself from touching her again. "I'd really counted on at least a four-night stand," he grumbled. And grinned sheepishly.

She reflected back the smile. "See you in the morning."

"See you." He about-faced and left her, disappearing into his room without looking back.

Charlie slipped into her own cheerless room. Nice going, she silently congratulated herself. Prude-of-the-year nominee.

She pitched into bed, licking her lips, imagining the taste of him lingered there. Resolutely, she closed her eyes and was soon asleep.

CHARLIE WOKE to the sound of bumping and banging. When she opened the door the width of her head, she found Ross piling backpacks and sleeping bags. Wearing a blue plaid shirt, hiking boots and jeans that had definitely shrunk to fit, he looked delightfully macho.

"Ready in a minute," she said, slamming the door and hurrying to keep the promise. She put on clothes similar to those Ross was wearing, and tamped the safari hat onto her hair. Carrying her camera and jacket, she walked into the hall.

Ross inspected her with the impersonal expression of a drill sergeant. "Is that the warmest coat you've got?"

When she nodded, he went into his room, then promptly came back carrying a puffy, royal-blue jacket. "This is down-filled. It's probably too big, but it'll feel good when the sun goes down."

A similar jacket was part of the stack of supplies on the floor. "Can two of us carry all that stuff up the mountain?"

"It's mostly air except for the food," he assured her curtly. "The climb is fairly steep, but there's plenty of time to reach the homestead before dark. We can stop and rest as often as you need."

Ross had breakfast ready on the keep-warm. He poured two cups of coffee and promptly fed two bread slices to the toaster. Charlie smiled to herself, thinking how right she'd been to resist his seduction the night be-

fore. He'd have been even more impossibly brisk and ef-
ficient this morning!

They loaded the van and backed into the shady street.
As Ross drove, taciturn, his eyes fixed on the road,
Charlie anticipated with satisfaction the adventure she'd
instigated, till it occurred to her that they were driving
east, away from the mountains.

Apprehensively, she studied Ross's expressionless
profile. "Uh, where are we going?"

"Unscheduled stop."

The timing was perfect. He immediately steered toward the curb in front of an apartment complex built to
mimic a ski resort—raw redwood planks, steep roofs
with dormers and chimneys, balconies loaded with firewood and bicycles.

When Ross opened the passenger door, Charlie
dropped to the pavement awkwardly, the weight of the
unfamiliar boots hastening her descent. He steadied her,
hand to elbow.

"First floor, center," he directed.

"Evan, I presume?" Maybe Ross believed her at last.

He grunted and punched the doorbell.

The opening wooden door shrieked at its badly fitted
frame, and Evan squinted out. Needing a shave and a
clean shirt, wearing a red pencil over one ear, he carried
some of his breakfast, a slice of pizza.

"Hey, I just tried to call you. Come in, come in. Want
a beer or a chair or a cup of sugar or what?"

"I want my grandmother's journal," Ross said, glancing around the untidy living room.

Books, clothing and food wrappers festooned the
Danish modern furniture. Charlie's eyes, skidding away
from an athletic supporter gracing a lampshade, met
Evan's bland smile.

"Son of a gun. You really can clairvoy." He bit off a mouthful of pasta. "Over here."

Walking to the dinette table, he pawed through heaped papers to uncover a well-worn, brown leather book. Swallowing, he said more plainly, "I must've picked it up with the exams yesterday in your office. Sorry, Boss." He handed it to Ross, who tucked it under his arm and began to shepherd Charlie to the door.

"Unbelievable." Evan jammed the last of the pizza into his mouth and dusted his hands. "You've convinced me, Charlie. Incredible. So now you're on your way to the high country to work your spells. Had any visions about it? What it is?"

Charlie shook her head. "Maybe once we're up there."

Evan swung the door wide for them. "See you in a couple of days. Happy hunting." He signed thumbs-up as they crossed the plank porch. "Bring me a ruby."

They rode in silence through midtown traffic, heading north, then west. The van began to climb, and Boulder disappeared behind them before Ross remarked, "That was quite impressive."

"Just my job," she said lightly, suspicious of his meaning.

"At the risk of rousing your ire, tell me one more time that you and Evan weren't coconspirators on this."

"One more time. Evan and I did not set you up. No. No. No."

He downshifted for an S-curve. "The journal's behind my seat if you want to see it."

"Not now." She smiled as he glanced at her. "I want to sightsee now. And examine the journal up at the homestead site."

"You're the expert."

Her smile broadened.

As the van caromed from curve to curve, spiraling higher, red rocks closed ranks to form a canyon. A shallow creek churned on Charlie's side. Wildflowers curtsied to the van's passage.

"Will there still be snow up where we're going?"

"There'll be pockets of it on north faces that don't get much sun. Probably not enough for a snowman. Unless you want to go higher than the homestead."

"What's up higher?"

"If you go far enough, you come to the summit of Meadow Mountain, which is in Rocky Mountain National Park. But that's a difficult five or six miles. The terrain immediately behind the homestead is similar to what we walked up on Sunday, only steeper. Half a mile up, there's a little lake called Sayers Lake, and another mile farther there's a bigger lake, both city-owned reservoirs."

They tooled along for a few minutes in comfortable silence.

"Charlie—" He hesitated. "I've been letting you railroad me into this adventure with all this crazy talk about treasure, but the truth is, even if we found something— a gold mine, say—it wouldn't help Mandy or me." Effortlessly he avoided a pothole. "I mean, the land doesn't belong to us. It's National Forest Service property. Unless the Sayers tiara is very portable and personal, like a ring with Grandmother's initials in it, we wouldn't get to claim it."

"I realize that. Mandy knows it, too. It was solving the mystery that intrigued both of us."

"Good. You're curious, not greedy."

"Right. There are treasures and there are treasures." She couldn't stop herself from glancing at his now familiar profile as she said it.

A tiny ground squirrel, legs churning furiously, crossed the road. Charlie's delighted giggle painted a smile on Ross's face.

"That's the first I've seen you smile all morning," she said.

"Sorry." Ross scrubbed the back of his neck with a palm. "I've been uptight, trying to remember what all we'd need, wondering about the journal, and—" he switched his attention from the road to her face just long enough to send a shiver to her core "—trying to forget my sexual deprivations."

Charlie pretended sudden interest in the green-and-white sign they were passing. "'Climb to safety in case of a flash flood.' Flood? That trickle of a creek?"

"That trickle can, under the right conditions, change this canyon into a conduit full of churning water, a wall of water as high as thirty feet. It's happened a couple of times in sister canyons in the last decade. A hundred people were killed in the Thompson Canyon flood, and Estes Park's business district had to rebuild after the dam at Lawn Lake burst, letting Fall River careen down the mountain."

"Is that what happens? A dam breaks? Isn't there an agency to inspect for deterioration?"

"What usually happens is there's a cloudburst in the high country that dumps a lot of water on a relatively small area in a short time, putting enormous strain on a dam. Sometimes the dam doesn't even break. It just can't contain the surplus water. And the ground can't absorb it fast enough."

"So it takes the path of least resistance, down a benign little creek bed like this one."

"Right. There're a lot of little lakes up here dammed at the turn of the century that aren't safe. They ought to be drained and returned to their natural state."

"I can't imagine meeting a thirty-foot wall of water here," Charlie marveled.

"Good. Don't."

They rode without speaking for several minutes, enjoying the scenery and each other's proximity. Ross's mood had, indeed, lightened. As he thought of Charlie's rejection the night before, he admired rather than resented it. The lady had willpower as well as brains and beauty! He couldn't help but anticipate that tonight would prove well worth the wait.

He started guiltily when Charlie said, "Tell me about your grandparents. When did they come to Colorado?"

"Grandmother was born here. Her dad was a blacksmith at Gold Hill when it was a going community. She was only seventeen when she married Timothy Sayers. The story goes, he'd been a hermit twenty-some years up here at the homestead site, living a quiet, hand-to-mouth existence with his own truck garden and livestock. And one day he chanced in at the Gold Hill General Store, laid eyes on Elizabeth, and, one month later, he brought her to his hideaway as his bride. They still lived hand-to-mouth, but the six children he sired permanently disrupted the quiet."

Charlie braced one hand on the dashboard as the van jounced across a rash of loose gravel. "Your mother was the youngest?"

He nodded. "Martha. Next youngest was Esther, my aunt whose *house*-pitality we currently enjoy. All the other siblings are gone, dead."

"How did Timothy and Elizabeth die?"

"He went first, in his sixties, from tuberculosis. Grandmother lived long enough to put the older daughters in charge of the younger ones, and then she caught a flu that turned into pneumonia. She was thirty-seven when it killed her."

"How sad, to have lived such a hard, short life."

"Yes, well, she probably didn't mind. In those days, in this part of the world, life was like that for almost everyone. Few modern conveniences. No wonder drugs. Bitter cold winters without electricity or running water."

"No electricity?" Charlie's side window had begun to rattle in time with the washboard road.

"Not at the homestead. Hey, you didn't pack your electric hair dryer, did you?"

"I didn't even bring my mascara. I don't want to lug anything up that grade unless it has at least two vital uses."

Ross gave her shoulder a companionable squeeze. "That rule ought to go into every camper's guidebook."

He let go, needing both hands to wrestle the steering wheel around a gully and into what Charlie recognized as the "parking lot" for their trail head.

The first thing Ross did when they'd bailed out of the van was offer Charlie a tube of suntan lotion. Next he fastened a water canteen to the rear right-hand belt loop of her jeans, relishing the intimacy of her hip cocked toward him. He helped her tie the borrowed jacket around her waist by the sleeves. Finally, he harnessed her into the backpack, taking extra time to examine the adjustments and the fit.

"Too heavy?" he asked.

"Nope. But if I fall on my back, promise you'll flip me over."

She watched him don his own gear. The backpack had two sleeping bags strapped across the top. "Whoa," she protested. "I forgot about sleeping bags. Let me carry my own."

"My treat," Ross assured her. "Unless," and he twirled the ends of an imaginary mustache, "you consent to leave one behind."

She laughed. "Oh, I couldn't do that. You'd probably have an awfully uncomfortable night, sleeping on the bare ground."

Groaning from her joke—or perhaps the weight of the pack he was shrugging into place, he slammed the van door, and set off. Charlie, thumbs under the straps of her pack, started to follow.

"Ross, have you got the journal?"

He half turned and patted his chest to indicate it was inside his shirt. Satisfied, she saved her breath for hiking.

At first, the awkwardness of the extra weight bothered Charlie. She clumped doggedly behind Ross, concentrating on lifting her feet high enough to clear the next rock riser. But as her body warmed, her motion began to piston more smoothly; she could look around and take pleasure in her surroundings, and enjoy the sight of Choke Creek, jigging down as they trudged up.

Ross led a steady but unhurried pace, seeming, in fact, to have forgotten Charlie, his stride lengthening as private thoughts engrossed him. Just when she decided she'd have to call for a break, Ross sat down on what she realized was the whale boulder and unsnapped his canteen.

"How're you doing?" He drank, wiped off the top, and offered it to her.

"I'm doing fine. But the worst is yet to come, I assume."

"It's rougher, but don't worry, we won't have to rope ourselves together."

She beat him to the next line. "Unless we want to be kinky. I know." She took two swallows of water and handed it back.

"You really are quite brave to come out here in the wilderness with me, with no one else around for miles." Ross stoppered the canteen with a slap of his palm. "Well, maybe not brave. Maybe more like dumb."

Charlie leaned back on her stiffened arms, eyes closed, face absorbing the sun. "I'd like to think that if you treat a person as if you trust him, he'll behave in a trustworthy manner."

Ross snorted. "Or take you for everything you've got."

Charlie's mouth curved up. "I like you a lot, Dr. Davies." She opened one eye and caught him looking at his watch.

"Time-out's up," he announced brusquely. "On your feet. No more dawdling. Look lively."

What trail there was soon petered out. As the terrain roughened, Charlie had to resort to hand as well as footholds, scrambling up rock slides, clutching at bushes, her mouth dry from breathing through it. At intervals, she rested long enough to clear her buzzing head, while Ross waited patiently.

"Think how easy this will be going back tomorrow," he said once. A couple of stops later, he remarked, "Over half-way there." The next time Charlie paused, Ross made her laugh. "The Avon lady is buried around here somewhere."

She blotted her sweaty forehead on her shirtsleeve. "I'm sorry to slow you down this way. I feel as if my body weighs two hundred pounds and my head weighs an ounce."

"If you can flog yourself another twenty yards, there's a pretty little meadow where you can lie down and let me feed you grapes."

"I think I can, I think I can."

As they approached the last few feet to the lip of the plateau, Ross reached back to drag her up and over. She slumped against the nearest boulder and looked around at a natural cup of grassy land encircled by grotesque fingers of rock and shaggy evergreens.

"Wonderful," she pronounced, when she had enough breath to speak.

Ross freed the sleeping bags to use as overstuffed seating. He rummaged through both packs to assemble a cold lunch of turkey sandwiches, raw vegetables, cheese and the promised grapes.

"Drink as much water as you can," Ross advised. "To avoid mountain sickness. There's plenty more water at the cabin."

"How close are we to it now?" Charlie asked, realizing she sounded like a kid pestering her parent.

"Less than an hour away." Ross wadded up his sandwich wrapper and moved over to share her bedroll. "How's the new pair of clodhoppers?"

"Better than I expected. The heel of this one's rubbing, though."

The tops of their heads brushed as they bent to remove Charlie's right boot. Ross stripped off the sock and gently angled her foot to see the heel.

"And you thought 'Dr. Davies' was just a title of respect," he said, searching Charlie's pack for the first-aid pouch.

He applied gauze and tape, squeezing her ankle affectionately before handing her the sock. Charlie had never before thought of her foot as an erogenous zone.

"Does this plateau have a name?"

Ross stood up and prowled the clearing, nibbling at the last sprig of grapes. "I don't know its official name, but Mandy and I used to call it The Front Desk."

Charlie laughed. "Front desk as in hotel?"

"A fleabag, unfortunately. No bellboy. No elevator."

"Did you come up here often when you were children?"

"My father used to bring us up four, five times a year. Mother wasn't much interested in climbing a mountain just because it was here. I was sixteen when he died, so I could have started coming on my own, but I didn't get around to it very often. The last time was September. With Evan and some other graduate students for an ecology field trip. Actually it was just an excuse to play hooky on a spectacular autumn day. Ready to go?"

"I haven't seen any poison ivy," Charlie said, struggling to put on her pack.

"Too dry for it." His arms encompassed her, as he helped to seat the weight; it seemed to require considerable adjustment.

"Well, there's got to be something bad about this idyllic place," Charlie insisted.

"Rock slides. Snow avalanches. Floods. Killer squirrels."

"Killer squirrels?" She snickered and tipped her head to see his expression.

"The wildlife sometimes carries bubonic plague."

Charlie glanced at the ground involuntarily.

"Oh, yeah, and tonight," Ross continued, "we need to examine each other's bodies. For ticks."

She backed away from him, laughing.

"No, really!" he exclaimed. "Rocky Mountain spotted fever. Ticks are carriers." He held up two fingers in scout's honor.

"Boy, am I sorry I asked," Charlie muttered, scooping up her hat and pushing it over her hair.

The sun that had felt so good when they were resting, scorched their shoulders and drew sweat as they climbed. Under the cummerbund of down jacket, Charlie's midsection was wet; undoubtedly this could do wonders for one's figure.

They came to an aerie of rock. Like the turret of a castle, it afforded a magnificent view of the way they'd come, the surrounding mountains, and, through a conveniently placed valley, the eastern plains.

"This was our spy hole," Ross said, guiding Charlie to a fault between two boulders. Putting her eye to the crack, she could see The Front Desk, two stories below. She imagined what she and Ross would have looked like from up here—two dolls walking and talking and eating.

"Nice place for an Indian ambush," she said.

"There're plenty of places like that."

"Why did your ancestors want to live in such an inaccessible area?"

Ross waved his arm like a tour guide. "Look at this. If you had a mate and enough to eat and one change of clothes, and you could whittle, would you need the real world?"

Charlie considered. "I'd need a hot fudge sundae once, maybe twice a year. And magazines. But otherwise—oh, and the Chicago Bears. I'd miss them."

"All of them? No wonder you scare me," Ross mocked.

They shared the last of Charlie's canteen before getting on with the rest of their journey.

In an indecently brief space of time, Charlie's head was throbbing in rhythm with her booming heart. Her legs wobbling, she staggered behind Ross, trying to still the snuffles and gasps that her breathing had become. They rounded a shadowed corner and had to detour a spill of old snow.

Glimpsing Charlie's pale face, Ross took her hand to lead her to a sunlit boulder low enough for them to sit on.

"What a wimp," she finally managed to say.

"Are you addressing me, madam?" Ross feigned indignation.

She laughed. "I guess I am. You sat down first." She shut her eyes, which weren't focusing properly, and laid her head against his upper arm. "I hope your grandfather's treasure is a feather bed."

Ross gazed down at her, pleasure quirking his lips. "I wouldn't touch that line with an eleven-foot pole." Gently he eased her head onto his chest, freeing his arm to hug her shoulders. Her backpack made it awkward.

They sat still for so long, he suspected she'd fallen asleep, but then she asked, "What happened to your father?"

"He drowned." Ross stiffened his back and Charlie pushed away from his chest. "You're going to be sore tomorrow, Ms. Yost. You could, of course, persuade me to massage your limbs to minimize the discomfort."

She flapped a weak hand, the dizziness mildly erotic now.

"Torso too," he said. "Definitely should be massaged. No extra charge."

"I've heard of men plying women with alcohol to speed up the seduction, but I'd never have guessed high altitude could be used in a similar fashion." She did feel drunk.

"Don't pass out yet. Half a block to go, Charlie. You can do it. It was all your idea, remember. I don't want to say I told you so, but I told you so."

"That's it, get me mad. Pump me with adrenaline to drive me over the hump."

"Okay, last resort. I didn't want to have to do this, but I'm going to have to rape you."

"What?" Charlie screeched as his arm snugged up under her chin.

"God knows it's not going to be fun for me, but duty calls. Take off your clothes." He was bear-hugging her so that she couldn't have obeyed if she'd wanted to.

"Race you to the top," she gurgled.

Their roughhousing irritated a resident crow, whose squawk was a fair imitation of Charlie's.

"You shouldn't be resisting me," Ross puffed. "You need all your energy for the trail."

She immediately went limp, and, as she'd expected, he didn't know what to do with her. After trying unsuccessfully to hitch her dead weight into his lap, he draped her carefully over the boulder, and then she sensed him going away.

Peeping from one eye, she discovered him returning with a double handful of snow. Shutting the eye, lying in wait, her lips poised to smile, Charlie heard his breathing, and just as he bent over her, she straight-armed his hands and the snow into his own face.

Sputtering and shaking his head, Ross grabbed at her as Charlie, giggling, rolled off the boulder's other side. Clutching the pack harness to minimize wobble, she started uphill. Ross backtracked for more snow, giving her an extra ten steps of lead, and he was careful not to catch her till they reached the Sayers homestead.

Whereas The Front Desk covered less than an acre of meadow, this property was at least twice the size. The rough plank cabin stood well back, under the lip of a red cliff. As Charlie crossed the broad expanse in front of it, she saw evidence of life in the form of a garden—wild onions, lettuce, carrots and other hardy sprouts, elbowing through the dirt. Ten feet from the front entry—a cavity with no door—Charlie stopped, panting, to wait for Ross.

He was whistling "The Happy Wanderer," swinging a branch that had nearly tripped him in the final stages of the climb. He coasted to a stop beside Charlie and shielded his eyes to look around the clearing.

"Well, it's still here."

"Was there much danger of it not being here?" Charlie asked. "You surely don't have to worry about vandals."

"Vandals we have always with us. There's a charred spot on the back corner where some idiot tried to burn the cabin down. But nature is what vandalizes it most dramatically. Snow. Wind. Gravity."

On the right north side, a stand of five scruffy evergreens overhung the gabled roof. The first in line had sent a branch toward the doorway, as if to bar it. Ross swayed the limb aside and stepped across the threshold. Charlie stooped to peer beneath his arm.

The gloomy interior, about fifteen by twenty feet, was bare of everything but dirt. Two windows, one rock fireplace, one bird's nest in the rafters—that was it.

"How could eight people have lived in this little space?" Charlie wondered.

Ross moved into the room and pointed over the doorway. "The kids slept in a loft."

Suddenly aware of her backpack, Charlie shrugged it off and left it by the door, along with the down coat. The loft was a crude platform running the width of the building and protruding into the room.

"The ladder's missing," Ross explained.

The raw plank flooring, creased into traffic patterns by the feet of many Sayerses, crackled as Charlie went to the hearth. "Please, could I have the journal now?" she asked, noticing two depressions in the floor that had to have been made by a rocking chair.

"Don't you want to wait till later? Rest up first?"

"I may not see anything the first time I try. It could take awhile, so I want to get started."

Ross unbuttoned his shirt and brought out the diary. As she grasped it, Charlie tried to ignore the exposed line of male chest an arm's length away. The book felt warm.

Ross waited for her to look up at him. "Charlie, it isn't too late to change your mind. I won't be disappointed if you say you can't do this. I don't want you to feel bad when the vibes don't vibe, or whatever it is that's supposed to happen."

"When you have such confidence in me, how can I fail? Why don't you go refill the canteens or something? Leave me alone. Please."

"There's nothing in there that suggests where to find the Sayers tiara."

"I'm not going to read it. I'm going to hold it."

Ross snapped his fingers. "Why didn't I think of that." To soften the remark, he touched his mouth to her fully clothed shoulder, an extremely chaste kiss.

He left, dragging their gear with him.

5

CRADLING THE JOURNAL against her chest, Charlie toured the room; her free hand lightly explored dusty surfaces—the cool, grainy rock of the fireplace, splintered windowsills, a knothole in the door frame. The cabin creaked around her, and the sentinel tree tapped its branch against the window.

Returning to the hearth, she stooped to touch the indentations the rocking chair had made, and a vision arced across her mind with the evanescence of a flashbulb—a young woman breast-feeding an infant, each studying the other with open admiration. Smiling, Charlie glanced at the scarred brown book against her own breast before sitting on the edge of the low hearth to open it.

The tiny cursive's vertical strokes had a uniformly parallel slant, the margins were ruler-straight, and nothing had been crossed out or written over. It was the work of an artist.

But not the work of a writer, Charlie found as she began—in spite of what she'd told Ross—to read. *Planted 4 rose corn. Edna sik and burdok tea help.* No dates. It must have been hard to keep track of days in this hermitage.

Elizabeth used *T* to denote her husband. *T cut a ceder by the wash for kinling and his peple.* Charlie puzzled this out to mean Timothy had felled a tree for firewood and for whittling.

There was no distinction between great and small events. A son's falling from the loft and breaking an arm received the same number of sentences in the same laconic style as did the airing of the mattresses. Turning to the final entry, Charlie found the one reference to Timothy's riches. *They buried T's tresure this day.* Backtracking to previous pages, she found no clue as to whom "they" might be. For whatever reason, the journal ended, leaving ten blank pages.

Charlie closed the book and her eyes, emptying her mind.

ROSS WAS THINKING ABOUT Charlie. He had checked the cistern and found it full of water passable for washing. Then he'd taken the canteens to the creek, to fill them from a deep pool below the turbulent stretch he and Mandy had christened Rapid Falls. Stray droplets on his skin were so cold they seemed to burn.

He returned to the clearing with dead wood in the crook of one arm. There had been various camp-fire sites over the years. He hunkered down beside what appeared to be the most recent, a blackened circle of rocks halfway between cabin and creek, and began to construct a fire, all the while thinking about Charlie.

He pictured her in the cabin, her sweet face a mask, emotionless, while she looked at things no one else could see. That scared him, the weirdness of it. And of course it scared him that he cared for her, maybe even loved her, after knowing her less than four days.

Ross glanced at his watch and then at the sky. The mountains had swallowed the sun, leaving about five hours of cool daylight. He stared across the yard at the cabin doorway, and, as if he'd conjured her there, Charlie appeared. She strolled toward him. A gust of breeze wrapped her hair across her face, hiding her shy smile. When she lifted her arm to pull aside the wisps, the graceful line of her body made Ross's ache with longing. He had an overwhelming urge to run, but whether it was to or away from her, he couldn't have said.

She stopped an arm's length off and held out the journal.

"Any luck?" he asked.

"I saw your beautiful grandmother, but nothing else yet."

Ross tapped the book against his thigh. "When you *see* people, do you—can you talk to them?"

"Not 'talk' the way you mean it. There sometimes seems to be a telepathy, when they seem to be communicating what they're thinking to me."

"Are they aware of you being there?"

Charlie ran her hands into the back pockets of her jeans and frowned at her toes. "I don't know. If I think a question, I may think an answer, and it's possible the answer could be coming from them."

"Ahhh!" Ross startled her, throwing up his arms. "I can't believe I'm seriously entertaining the thought that there's any validity to ESP. It's crazy. There's no logical explanation for it."

"There's no explanation for gravity, either, but you don't question it exists. You can't explain human memory, but it certainly exists." She hunched her shoulders and shivered. "Someone turned down the thermostat."

Ross dipped into their supplies and tossed her the blue jacket. "Want to see a waterfall?"

"Oh, boy!" She freed her hair from the jacket collar and gave her hand to Ross.

They walked toward the creek, comfortably silent. Turning upstream along the brushy bank, they dropped hands to go single file. The steepness of the grade and the noise of the water intensified until, rounding a gigantic boulder, they could see the falls. It was a modest drop, about six feet, but the white water churning over the flat rock shelf to foam in the pool below was fairy-tale pretty.

Charlie had grabbed her camera on the way, and putting Ross into different poses, she snapped several photographs. Then he used the camera to take pictures of her, and then they wasted four frames trying to remember how to time-delay a photo with both of them in it. On the fifth try, the camera whirred while they held breaths, smiles and each other's waists, like school chums.

"That's probably a great shot of our knees," Charlie said, collecting the camera from the boulder they'd used as a tripod.

"Gee, I hope so. Knees are my fetish." He stopped her with a hand on her arm, but it was only to point at the edge of the pool. "We can get fresh water over by that stepping-stone."

"Is it safe to drink the water before boiling it first?"

"There's probably nothing between here and the glacier it's melting from to pollute it. Maybe some deer slobber."

Charlie rolled her eyes. "How can I take a swig now without thinking of that?"

"Seriously, we'll boil the water first, just to be sure it's safe." Ross pointed to the pine tree listing into their path. "Speaking of flavors, smell that. Not the needles, the trunk."

"Smell a tree?" Charlie repeated suspiciously. She put a supportive hand on the gnarled orange bark and leaned her nose to within an inch of it, rocked back to think, returned for a second whiff. "Strawberry. How odd. What kind of tree is this?"

"Ponderosa. The five up next to the cabin all smell like butterscotch. And some ponderosa have the aroma of vanilla."

Back at the cabin, the first thing Charlie wanted to do was sniff the trees along its north side. The breeze was becoming rowdier, prodding branches against the plank walls, making them squeal like fingernails on a blackboard.

"Hungry?" Ross asked.

"I could eat a butterscotch ponderosa."

Charlie wiped hair out of her eyes and watched Ross assemble the cooking equipment—coffeepot, skillet, wooden spoon, packets and tins of food. With his back to the wind, he crouched to light the fire, nursing it with handfuls of dry tumbleweed and twigs. When it was truly caught, he stepped back and looked across the flames at Charlie. She'd taken off the jacket, and her figure undulated in the heat waves.

"Anything I can do?" she asked.

Mesmerized, he shook his head, wishing he could tell her what he thought.

"Then do you mind if I just look around and—meditate?"

He shook his head again and pretended the fire needed emergency stoking. When she turned away, he studied the way her jeans hugged her hips. Then he knelt on one knee to wait for the flames to age to coals and his own localized burning to cool.

She followed the meadow's periphery past the remains of a haphazard stone wall and the foundation of what must have been a privy. She'd wrapped the down jacket around her shoulders when she'd left the fire. Now she slipped her arms into the sleeves, as the cool breeze leaped and died, leaped and died.

Reaching the rock cul-de-sac behind the cabin, she pivoted to examine that side of the building. The site of the attempted arson that Ross had mentioned looked like a dark bruise. The chimney stone had been sloughing off to litter the ground.

She moved into the windbreak of the rock cliff overhang. There had been several camp fires here. From this vantage, she could see Ross bending over what must be their supper cooking. In the shallow cavelike depression of the red wall, a trespasser had scratched modern hieroglyphs: LHS '80. At her feet, a pitiful heap of feathers and bones attested to one of nature's everyday dramas.

Charlie looked at Ross again. He was drinking from a cup. When he saw her looking at him, he raised it in salute.

Breathing deeply, she shut her eyes and concentrated on a pinpoint of light she'd willed into the darkness. The light grew, and like a traveler in a tunnel, her mind approached the glow, left the dark, emerged into a setting exactly like the real one she'd just left. Except Ross was gone. And something terrible was with her.

She searched for the menace, her thoughts raking the cliff face, the cabin wall, the expanse of meadow. No one, nothing showed itself while her heart battered inside her chest.

And then she was struck. She felt the claws sink in and her vertebrae snap. She heard the wings of the predator and sensed the spasms of her own soft feathers.

"No," she told herself sternly, ignoring pain. "Show me the treasure."

Like the fading houselights of a theater, her vision dimmed. After a moment, she looked down on the homestead meadow as she had earlier viewed The Front Desk from above. There was Ross, smaller than life, as if she were watching him through the wrong end of a telescope. Mentally pulling him closer, she saw the negligent angle of one long leg propped against a stump, the lean line of his torso, the corded neck. Closing in, she could make out the golden-stubbled jaw, the flash of teeth, the pupils expanding in his silver-flecked blue eyes.

Charlie repeated her silent incantation. "Show me the treasure."

And she slipped into his body, like a diver enveloped by a tropical lake. She floated languorously inside his skin, hearing his heartbeat, sharing his emotions of longing and lust.

"Charlie." His voice rippled past her ears. She pretended not to notice—a sleeper reveling in the dream—but he called louder. "Charlie, supper's ready."

Reluctantly she migrated to her own body and opened its eyes. Ross was motioning to her across the fire. Instead of taking the direct path past the cabin, she continued scouting the cliff toward Choke Creek and then along the southern perimeter of the clearing back to her starting point.

Ross noted her progress, hands on his hips, and chastised her when she was finally within earshot, "You can play after supper, young lady. You better come when I call, if you don't want it to get cold."

She sank down cross-legged on a bedroll. "I don't like spinach or coconut or liver."

"Fortunately I didn't make my famous spinach-coconut-liver casserole. Try this."

He handed her a plastic bowl steaming with the scent of tuna. He set a cup of coffee on the ground in front of her.

"Mmm. What is this stuff?" She licked her spoon appreciatively.

"One of those instant noodle dinners you get in a box, plus a little can of tuna fish. Plus a pinch of dirt when I dropped the stirring spoon."

"You'll have to make it exactly the same next time, dirt and all."

Ross sat on the other sleeping bag at right angles to Charlie's. "Did you have any psychic luck? See any treasure?"

"I saw treasure," she agreed, smiling at her private joke. "But it wasn't the right one."

Ross eyed her quizzically over the rim of his cup. "How do you know it wasn't Grandfather's treasure?"

"Because—" She lowered her spoon and gazed thoughtfully at the fire. "Actually it was a valuable that Grandfather Sayers was partly responsible for. I asked to be shown the treasure, and what I saw was you." She glanced sideways at him.

Ross continued to eat, elbows on knees, shoulders bunched. "So I guess you need to be more specific next time."

"Apparently. Is there time before the light's gone to go to Sayers Lake?"

"If you want to." The curtness of his answer rang in his own ears, making him realize how much he'd been dreading seeing Sayers Lake again. He forced a smile and a more hearty, "We can buzz up to the lake for a minute. We'll take the flashlight, just in case."

The breeze had shifted 180 degrees to sweep up from the east. Crisscrossing green branches to partially smother the fire, Ross said, "It'll be okay. We'll be able to see it most of the time from the trail and once we're on top by the lake."

"This little climb should be a cinch. We can negotiate the path like mountain goats instead of beasts of burden." Charlie pranced toward the path.

"The burden's just inside instead of outside now," he reminded her, rubbing his belly. "You really shouldn't go hiking for half an hour after you eat or you'll get cramps."

"Really?" She stopped in her tracks.

"Nah, I just made that up," he said, throwing an arm over her shoulder to draw her along in his stride.

They pushed and pulled each other up the incline in the rapidly dissolving daylight. When they reached the lake, it was a ghostly outline in the darker gray landscape. Covering about the same acreage as the homestead meadow, the water lapped high against the manmade dam enclosing the downslope side.

Charlie walked to the brink. "Is it deep?"

Ross didn't answer, and she pivoted to see why. He was motionless, lost in thought, hands loose at his sides.

But he'd heard the question. "It's V-shaped to the bottom," he said, "close to fifty feet deep at the middle."

"It's eerie in the twilight."

Ross stepped to the drop-off overlooking their campgrounds to check on the fire. "Did you know the word 'bonfire' comes from the Anglo-Saxon expression *bone fire*, meaning funeral pyre?"

"Is this to put us in the mood for ghost stories before bed? Speaking of bed—" she added, succumbing to a yawn.

"It's only eight forty-five," he objected.

"And? You have a program planned? If it requires anything more strenuous than keeping my eyelids up, forget it."

"No touch-football? Then I guess you don't want to climb another mile to Chokecherry Lake, either."

"Invite me again in the morning."

They needed the flashlight before they'd gotten halfway down to the meadow. The trail blacked out and the dome of gray overhead was still too pale for stars to show. Ross directed the ray of light in front of Charlie's feet, like an experienced movie usher. Once her boot skidded on a patch of loose dirt, and his sinewy arm flew around her waist to anchor her.

They slid and slithered down the final slope and crossed to the smoking camp fire.

"Is this where we put the sleeping bags?" Charlie asked.

"Unless you've got a better suggestion."

"Maybe I'd pick up more information if I slept in the cabin," she thought aloud. "But it's so lovely out here with infinity for a ceiling."

"That's a nice, poetic phrase." He broke a stick across his knee to add to the fire. The crack echoed off the cliff wall.

They prepared for sleep, taking turns going behind the cabin, washing in cold water. Searching out the smoothest place to position the sleeping bags, they unrolled them onto twin groundsheets.

"This is new to me," Charlie began shyly. "Is it okay to leave my clothes on?"

"Much as I'd like to say 'take them all off,' you'll probably want to wear everything but your boots. Just loosen your jeans and whatever else is tight, after you get into the sleeping bag."

Feeling self-conscious, Charlie worked her way into the down cocoon. Squirming to get into a more comfortable position, she forced shut her no longer sleepy eyes. "'Night."

She heard Ross's bag being dragged nearer. His feet tramped uncomfortably close to her head. Something thudded; a zipper whined.

"Charlie?" he said inches from her face.

Her eyes flew open. He'd put his sleeping bag head-to-head with hers, but he was half out of it, canting on one elbow to look into her upside-down face. The soft firelight danced in his eyes.

"Could we talk a minute?" he appealed.

"What about?" She'd been expecting—anticipating— a move like this.

"About what you said last night." Using his elbows, Ross pulled himself closer over to her, to touch her mouth and chin with his warm lips.

When she could get a word in edgewise, Charlie chided, "I thought you wanted to talk."

"Strictly speaking, what I want to do is get into your sleeping bag with you."

She sighed, exasperated and exhilarated at the same time. He seemed intent on covering every square inch of her face with butterfly kisses. The tour ended at her mouth again, to which he gave a thorough taste test.

When at last he raised his head, she made another shaky attempt to restore reason. "Ross, what was it you wanted to talk—repeat—*talk* about?"

Ross rolled onto his back and rested his head on Charlie's sleeping bag. His cheek was against her temple. "The way you kiss me, I'd say you like me," he murmured.

"Very much."

"There's nothing physically wrong with either of us."

"Not that I'm aware of."

"Good. That means there isn't. And this is the nineties."

"Last time I looked," she said when he seemed to be awaiting an answer.

"I mean, a woman can enjoy safe sex with a man she likes 'very much,' and she needn't feel stigmatized for life."

"Assuming her psychological profile permits that kind of social response."

"And who's to say we aren't going to see each other again? Our feelings could grow to the point we'd be willing to rearrange our lives to accommodate one another."

"Do you usually engage in a debate with the lady whom you wish to bed?" Charlie was struggling not to laugh.

"It was you who said we ought to talk! If it were up to me, I'd just get on with the important stuff." He turned his face to nuzzle her hairline. "So what do you say, Charlie?" His whisper tickled her neck. "If I promise to protect you from babies and speak to you civilly in the morning, will you let me do tender, passionate things to you tonight? Think about it for a minute." And he gently guided her chin toward him, his hand gliding down to massage the pulse in her throat.

"Ross," she tried to say against his mouth.

"Not yet," he said on hers. Continuing the kiss, he maneuvered himself out of his bag and stretched out on top of hers, pinning her down carefully, weight on his knees and elbows.

Eyes shut, Charlie was seeing tiny explosions of light. Caught up in the kiss, she drifted, a passive recipient at first, then more and more responsive. She whimpered, wanting to wrap her arms around Ross.

When he opened the sleeping-bag zipper, the tips of his fingers brushed her breast. Desire coursed through her.

Afraid to lift his head and let her speak, Ross prolonged the kiss and swayed slightly to one side to work the zipper lower, peeling the material away, letting cold air strike her already trembling body. His hand tunneled under her shirttail, under the bra she'd loosened for sleeping, and cupped her right breast. Involuntarily, her body arched.

Ross's dull ache flowered into urgent need. The sensation of her soft flesh against his palm and the unmistakable movement of her pelvis forced his head back in a reflexive groan.

"Ross," she was able to whisper. "I don't think this is—" She gasped as he pinched her traitorous nipple, sending little stabs of excitation directly to her groin.

"Ross," she tried again, feeling him push her shirt and bra out of the way. His hair brushed her chin as he lowered his face to her chest.

"Ross!" It came out as a yelp when his warm lips and careful teeth found their mark.

Her eyes were wet now with tears of ambivalent emotion. She wanted him. She needed his hard body to cover her and fill her and stroke her to release. But she was also afraid. Not of Ross. Of something else.

Ross's relentlessly tender mouth and hands distracted her, and she had to make him stop so that she could *see*. With a twist so violent it scraped his teeth across her skin, Charlie threw herself sideways and curled into a protective ball.

"My God, Charlie," he choked. "Don't do this to me."

"Wait!"

His reaching hand turned palm up in supplication.

"Wait," she repeated. "Please don't say anything and don't touch me." Her mouth felt swollen, slurring the words. "I need to concentrate."

With one frustrated oath, Ross surged to his feet and went to kick the fire.

A chilly breeze dried the sweat from his skin, and he shivered. Looking over his shoulder at Charlie, he was torn between longing to caress her and needing to yell at her. She lay mummylike, arms crossed to hold her shirt closed, skin mottled by shadows and firelight.

Without opening her eyes, she said, "We aren't alone."

Swearing again, Ross planted his feet apart and dashed sticks at the fire. "Don't you pull that supernatural mumbo-jumbo on me. If you don't want to make love, just say so."

"It's true. There's someone else or something else in the meadow with us, hostile to us." Her eyes batted open, unfocused with alarm.

A new idea dawned on Ross. He squatted in front of her and asked gruffly, "Is it your first time? You don't need to be afraid. We'll take it very, very slow."

"You aren't listening!" she cried, sitting up and twitching her clothes into place. "I'm telling you we're in some kind of danger. I can't relax enough to see what it is."

Bitterly disappointed, Ross rose and returned to stare into the fire. His sad voice wafted back to her. "You're so beautiful. Warm and funny and smart. But this obsession with the supernatural cancels out all the pluses. ESP is going to ruin you." He swiveled from the knees to study her. "It's a helluva shame."

"You're handsome and warm and funny and smart, too," she recited. "But you're riddled with self-righteous skepticism. You arrogantly shut your ears and mind, and you hypocritically accuse *me* of not listening to reason!" Her voice hardened as her anger kindled to the attack. "You're the classic example of snicker effect—you only pick out events and facts that support your disbelief, and you ignore all the events and facts that might make you change your mind."

Ross stalked to his rumpled sleeping bag and jammed his legs inside. "It's bad enough that you'd lead me on till I can scarcely control myself, but then to panic and back out when you have me so aroused and blame it on a psychic vision, that's contemptible."

"I led you? Who was it worming into my sleeping space when I was half-asleep? Who held me down and smeared me with kisses and tried to feel me under my clothes?"

"'Tried?' I did feel you. And you loved it. Till your prudish instincts won out over your better nature. And then—I can't get over how devious you are—you start caterwauling about an evil menace about to get us."

Charlie lay down and worked the zipper of the bag upward to her chin. "There's no use arguing with an opinionated mule. If nothing horrible happens to us tonight, I'll see you in the morning."

Ross didn't answer. In his estimation, something horrible had already happened. He was miserable, physically and mentally in turmoil. He settled into the sleeping bag and stared at the star-freckled sky. Gradually he relaxed enough to sleep.

Charlie had finally drifted into sleep, too.

She knew it was a dream, this floating, swimming sensation. The scene was blurred, like being in a car going through a car wash. Water sheeted, cascaded around her, and she heard muffled slaps and gurgles. A figure glided at her, limbs performing a slow ballet, mouth shaped in an O to match the widened eyes, a sluggish hand rising to point. It was Ross.

Before she could reach out to him, a gushing swarm of bubbles covered his head. When the froth cleared, two metallic fish darted hide-and-seek in the empty sockets of his eyes.

"No!" Charlie screamed.

Her eyes snapped open. She heard rustlings and scrapings as someone scuttled in her direction. When strong hands ripped at the sleeping-bag fastener, she screamed again and went limp as Ross scooped her forward against his chest, murmuring reassurances. She clung to his shirtfront and pressed her nose into his neck.

"Okay now?" he asked.

"It was you," she tried to explain without crying. "You were drowning."

A muscle in his jaw tightened. He gazed across Charlie's shoulder at the specter moon hovering over the cliff wall. "Shh. It was only a bad dream."

"But it was *my* dream," she pointed out, and he understood that she meant it might have psychic significance.

"Charlie, it wasn't me you saw." He tightened his embrace and gave her a slight shake. "It wasn't me."

"It was! Your hair, your eyes, your mouth, you."

"It was my father."

She caught her breath and let it out in a slow sigh. "You told me he drowned."

"That's right, I did. You forgot it, but your subconscious was still mulling it over." He felt her relax. "What I didn't tell you was that it happened here."

"Oh, no, Ross. I'm so sorry."

"He used to come up to Sayers Lake to fish off the banks. Sometimes he'd bring me along, sometimes he'd take a buddy or two. This trip it was him and an old friend, who didn't see my dad fall into the lake. Most likely it was a misstep on a wet bank. He was fully clothed, and the water was frigid, and he may have hit his head. The friend couldn't swim, and he said Dad never resurfaced."

Ross straightened one leg to ease a cramp before he continued. "For a long time I couldn't bear to come up here. I blamed myself, thinking I could have saved him somehow. Which is nonsense, of course."

"And normal," Charlie murmured.

Ross released her to look at his watch. "Almost 2:00 a.m." He raked his fingers through his hair and rolled to his feet.

She cleared her throat and said, "Ross?"

"Yes?" he asked warily, determined not to expose himself to her refusals a third time.

"Please, could you just hold me a while? I'm so cold and still afraid, and it would be such a comfort to lie against you."

"Nothing else? You want me to sleep with you and just—sleep?"

She nodded. "Wouldn't you like that better than being over there by yourself?"

"Do you know what torture it would be for me to be that close to you and no closer? You must think I'm made of asbestos. No. No, Charlie, I want to be alone."

He stamped away three steps, stared down at his sleeping bag for half a minute, whipped it up over one arm and stamped the three steps back to her. He sighed heavily. "Move over," he ordered grumpily.

Trying to wriggle sideways—impossible in the confining space—she yanked at the zipper to open the bag to him. He grunted, settling in next to her and drawing his open bag across them for cover. She raised her shoulders, inviting him to slide an arm around her, then burrowed her head into his chest. He breathed the clean scent of her hair and tried to think sobering thoughts.

"Thank you," she whispered.

"How do you expect to escape this straightjacket if something does come after us?" he growled.

"Go to sleep, Ross. I'll wake you in plenty of time."

"You're going to keep watch all night?"

"My subconscious will."

"Whew, that's certainly a load off *my* mind," he sneered.

"I knew you'd say something like that. Someday I'll convert you. Someday you'll apologize for being so thickheaded."

"What I'd like to know is, if you read the past, how come you thought I was going to drown? And how could you claim there's some kind of threat to us here in the meadow?"

"The past is my specialty. But a psychic can never ignore a dream or a flash of intuition, because it might have a meaning."

"Yeah, it means a cop-out when you don't want to do something," Ross observed gloomily. "Not tonight, Ross, I have a karma-ache."

"That's not fair." She tried to sit up, but there wasn't room. "If you would have asked me politely instead of vaulting on top of me, I'd have told you just as politely that it didn't seem like a good time for it because I felt very strongly that there was someone or ones here besides us, and I don't care for the idea of sex with an audience, especially if the audience is in some way hazardous to—"

"Shut up," he interjected quietly but firmly. "I'm going to sleep. My arm already is."

They both lay open-eyed, holding very still, aware of all the pressure points where their bodies met. Charlie could hear Ross's heartbeat slow down, and she felt her own adjust to match it. She half expected to begin purring.

His drowsy voice grumbled, "A lesser man would rape you."

She smiled against his shirtfront, knowing it was true.

After perhaps fifteen minutes, Ross began the slow, heavy breathing indicative of sleep. Charlie, satisfied that she could move now without igniting any fires, carefully eased her right leg over his body and straightened a tingling arm.

She'd been thinking about the anxiety that had made her rebuff his seduction. It wasn't caused by any fear of intercourse; she meant it when she'd boasted she wasn't afraid of Ross Davies. And she wasn't a virgin. The indecently handsome music major who'd overawed her for exactly one semester during her freshman year had taken care of that.

She tried to relive the moment that she'd deviated from the heat of single-minded sexual desire to the coldness of unfocused fright. What had she heard or smelled or tasted in the air? Asking herself for help, she closed her eyes and waited. It was dark there, an unrelieved blackness that lasted so long she forgot her quest and fell asleep.

6

CHARLIE'S FIRST, irrational thought—that she was paralyzed—panicked her. When her eyes darted open, they focused on a dimpled chin, inches away, and she went slack in Ross's restraining arms. Carefully raising her head, she peered around.

The sky shone gray-white in expectation of the coming sun. A blue jay in the ponderosa by the cabin was tongue-lashing something that had crossed him. The fire had dwindled to ashes.

Extricating herself from Ross and the sleeping bag was like the proverbial fat lady and girdle. Charlie didn't expect to escape without a fight, but Ross was obviously a heavy sleeper. Only a mumbled protest showed he noticed her leaving. She grinned at his oblivious, deceptive innocence.

Straightening up in the cold mountain air, she hurriedly put on jacket and boots. As she tramped toward the cabin, the jay burst into the sky and flapped away. She reconnoitered around the corner and found nothing to explain his temper tantrum. Before crossing the threshold into the musty interior, she let her pupils get accustomed to the bad light, then went to sit on the hearth.

She practiced respiration exercises and summoned the treasure. Nothing happened. She didn't see or feel anything. Minutes filed past. Frustrated, she changed her mantra from "Where is the treasure," to "*What* the hell is it then?"

Again, nothing. Again, time went its relentless way, and all she saw was the decrepit room around her. Eyes shut, she made a determined effort to relax, continued the vigil, and viewed the inside of her eyelids, nothing more.

She wanted the information too much. It was true that skepticism could block psychic ability. Ross's disbelief was literally driving her to distraction. She must—*must*—find the treasure to win his respect.

Disheartened, she paced in front of the fireplace, boots thumping hollowly. She braced an arm on the chimney and leaned her face into the crook of her elbow.

Darkness. Gradually, with a sense of déjà vu, Charlie saw sheeting water and heard the bubbling in her ears. She recognized her own whimper of apprehension as the swimmer appeared. With morbid fascination, she studied the man's face, so like Ross's—blue eyes, blond hair and the same endearing dimpled chin. But his nose was broader, his hairline higher, and his finger, raised to point, was missing the first joint.

She didn't want to see him dying again. Like a commuter lunging for a bus, Charlie threw herself away from the vision by concentrating on the foot she always left anchored in the real world. Slumped against the cabin wall, she let her pulse slow.

She'd never before had a paranormal experience that reinforced a sleeping dream. It had to mean more than a subconscious replay of the nightmare she'd had. She scrubbed her forehead, feeling dizzy with speculation.

Perhaps she could visit the lake again, now, by herself. Without the encumbrance of Ross's negative thoughts. From the cabin doorway, she decided he was still asleep, and she picked her way quietly across the yard to the short, steep path.

The jay had begun a fresh tirade somewhere higher. The only other sound was her labored breathing. One clumsy step dislodged a trickle of red gravel that whispered down the hill. Once she backslid a couple of feet before a handful of a sharp-bladed grass braked her.

She breasted the top, where the path divided around the lake. Choosing the left branch, she strolled, hands in pockets, shoulders hunched against the cold breeze. The gray water was a windowpane to a copycat world of red rock walls and lazily swaying grass streamers. She half expected a skeletal hand to emerge, truncated forefinger pointing.

After having made a complete circuit of the lake, she cautiously approached the edge close enough to stoop and touch the surface. Feet firmly planted, she resolutely plunged one hand into the cold water, so numbing it made her arm ache to the elbow. The next thing she felt was a pull, neither strong nor frightening, but a drawing sensation, a take-my-hand-and-follow-me summons as unmistakable as it was silent.

Tell me about the treasure, she begged in corresponding silence. *Please.*

Her hand sucked deeper and then bobbed up. She brought it dripping into her lap and stared at it. And then she tipped back her head to laugh. Scrambling upright, she danced toward the cliff overlooking the homestead.

Ross was out of the sleeping bag trying to coax the fire into life so that they could cook their breakfast on it.

"Hey," Charlie shouted, doing jumping jacks a yard from the drop. "Ross! Hey, Ross! I found it!"

He cupped his hands around his mouth and shouted something containing the words "damn fool" and "splat."

"Don't come up, I'll come down!" Charlie shrieked.

Alternately shuffling and hopping to footholds, she descended, anticipating what she'd say to Ross. She'd gone a fourth of the way down when, taking a bouldered corner at a speed bordering on reckless, she sensed movement in front of her and looked up in time to gasp before careening into the arms of a stranger.

Braced against another boulder, he took her weight with a muffled grunt. Her screech of surprise stuck in her throat as he clamped a chapped hand over her mouth. There was a brief, hushed scuffle until he had successfully tucked Charlie under one arm and wedged her between his hip and the rock. They rested a moment, his hand still mashing her mouth, the other hand pinching her wrists together.

He coughed in her ear and said, "I'm not going to hurt you."

Charlie thought it was too late to promise that. Her skin had been scraped in several places by his fingernails, and the pressure of his dirty hands stung the cuts.

"Mmm," she agreed, wondering how long it had been since he'd washed the palm pressing against her teeth.

"I'm going to let go your mouth. But if you say anything—" He let the imagined punishment build in her mind before detaching his fingers from her jaw. "I got something to show you."

She mentally groaned as he reached toward his jeans. When he whipped out a hunting knife, she actually felt relief.

"You do exactly what I tell you. No argument. Got that?"

She bobbed her head once, and he set her away from him and slowly let go of her wrists. Backed against the boulder, Charlie took steadying breaths and recognized his face.

Like his body, it was angular and narrow. A nest of waxy black hair leaked out around a navy-blue ski cap. Twin black caterpillarlike eyebrows nearly met over a long, lumpy nose. His stubbled cheeks were etched with exertion and old acne scars. His thin lips turned down toward a lantern jaw, as if trained that way by a life of disappointments.

He grimaced at her, showing perfect, dazzling white teeth. The last time, in Ross's office, he'd said, "I'm Cid." This time he said, "I thought you could predict stuff. Didn't you see me waiting in ambush, hah?"

She shook her head. "I had other things on my mind."

"Yeah, I know. The treasure. You know where it is now?"

The more he talked, the younger he looked. She guessed he was in his early twenties. "Could we go somewhere more comfortable to chat?" she asked.

"In a minute we're going down there with the professor. Let's be sure you understand the situation first."

"Good. Explain it to me. I certainly don't understand it yet." Arms folded, she regarded him with undisguised dislike.

"You're going to tell me where the fortune is, and I'm going to tie the two of you up and take it."

Charlie amended his age to sixteen. "That's dumb. Even if I told you where it is, I couldn't tell you what it is. Maybe it isn't portable. And even if you can carry it in one hand, how far do you think you could get with stolen treasure? It might be—probably is—too unique to fence or pawn."

Cid was shaking his head, smirking at her naïveté. "I'll figure something out. You just lead me to it."

Hallooing from below indicated Ross believed Charlie should have reached camp by now.

Cid jerked the knife. "Tell him you're coming."

"I'm coming, Ross!" she shouted obediently. "In a minute."

"So now tell me real fast. Where is it?"

She stuck out a belligerent chin. "It isn't mine to give away. You'll have to talk to Ross."

"Oh, for crying out—he doesn't know where it is."

"He will pretty soon. As soon as you let me go down there and tell him."

"Tell me now or not at all," he said with an oddly chilling inflection. He might be young, but he was dangerous, with the unpredictability of someone deeply disturbed.

Charlie wrapped her jacket tightly under her chin. "It's in the lake. I don't know what it is, but it's in the lake."

"Charlie!" Ross's voice sounded halfway up the path.

Both of them jumped and turned grim faces toward the sound. A moment later, Ross rounded a ledge and shaded his eyes at them.

Charlie's impulse was to launch herself at him, knives and precipices be damned. He looked so strong and handsome and capable, she was certain he could handle Cid.

But Cid threw out a wiry arm, trapping her where she stood. With exaggerated pantomimes, he showed Ross the knife. Ross froze, palms up, a negotiator showing good faith.

"What's going on?" he asked, only the gruffness of his voice indicating his emotion.

Cid pointed at Charlie with his chin. "The psych here is giving away your treasure."

"Charlie, are you okay?"

She had been till his concern radiated up to her. She had to nod; she'd have choked on words.

"Okay, Doc, you go on down to camp and stand out by the camp fire where we can see you when we come down, Charlie and I and the knife. Understand?"

Ross retreated a few steps, riveting Charlie with looks meant to reassure her before he turned and disappeared.

"Make some noise!" Cid shouted. "Whistle something."

An asthmatic version of "The Happy Wanderer" floated to them from farther and farther away.

"Now you," Cid ordered, stepping aside enough to let Charlie past. She slipped and slithered down at high speed, pursued by a single demon who, when they'd nearly reached bottom, snatched her arm and made her wait as he listened for Ross.

"Come ahead," Ross called. "I'm by the fire just like you told me to be."

Rushing toward Ross, Charlie expected to be hauled to a stop before she got there. It felt wonderful when Ross's strong arms pulled her into his chest and she could cling to him, hiding from Cid.

"Do I know you?" Ross's voice rumbled above her ear.

"Nobody knows me," Cid bragged. "Call me Cid. Not *S-i-d*, *C-i-d*. It's a nickname."

"I do know you. You're Evan's roommate."

"Ex. Ex-roommate. We have irreconcilable differences." Cid prowled the camp, attention divided between watching his prisoners and taking an inventory of their gear.

"What do you say we make some coffee?" Ross took a step toward the fire, towing Charlie with him.

"No! No boiling liquids to throw in my face. You think I'm an idiot? Sit down over there."

They sat on a rolled-up sleeping bag.

"Put your hands on your knees and keep them there." Cid crouched to hack at the straps of a backpack, producing, in moments, four pieces. "Okay, Charlie, tie his hands and feet."

She did it fast, certain Cid would yell at her for tying Ross's hands in front instead of back. But when she was through, Cid's only concern seemed to be for tightness. He trussed Charlie, giving Ross smirking, sidelong looks while he did it. Then he rifled Ross's pockets, transferring money and a folding knife he found there to his own. Satisfied that he had everything under control, Cid strutted off toward the creek.

As soon as he disappeared into the trees, Ross studied Charlie. "You sure you're okay?"

"He just scared me to death is all."

"Try not to make him angry enough to gag us. I want to be able to communicate with you at all times." He leaned to give her a fast, friendly kiss. "In a variety of ways." He shook his tethered wrists glumly. "I haven't figured him out yet."

"He's a little crazy."

"He's a lot crazy, wasting his time on a goofy heist where he doesn't even know what the loot is." After a moment of thought he added, "What is the loot?"

"I haven't the faintest idea," Charlie sighed. Then she smiled into Ross's eyes. "But I know it's in the lake!"

"Mmm," he said noncommitally.

"Come on, don't you believe it? My psychic talent finally paid off." She bumped shoulders with him playfully.

"Mmm."

"You don't believe it," she accused.

"Oh, I think there's a strong likelihood it's in the lake."

"Well, then? What's the problem?"

"I don't think your so-called psychic talent told you, that's all." Ross squinted across the meadow as if he were wishing Cid would come back to interrupt this discussion.

"I see," Charlie said evenly. "That is, I see in the accepted sense of the word *see*."

"Don't be angry, Charlie. What's wrong with using a high intelligence quotient and deductive reasoning to figure out that the tiara is in the lake? It is the logical place. You don't have to be psychic to work that out."

"Are you saying you've thought the treasure was in the lake all along?" Her stiffened shoulder was at least six inches away from his by this time.

"Well, no. But it sounds good now that you've figured it out, though."

"I didn't figure it out! I found it psychically. Something took my hand and said, 'Here it is.'"

"Shh, okay," Ross soothed, infuriating her even more.

Absorbed in their disagreement, they didn't notice Cid's return until he laughed. "Having a little spat, are we? Another one like last night? 'Oh, darling, don't do that,'" he falsettoed. "'No, no, it's evil.' And Doc goes, 'Shut up, my dearest, or I'll have to take you by force.'"

Charlie's indignation at Cid's distortion of their words was followed by a graver realization. "You were here last night. It was you I felt."

"Well, no, honey, I didn't have the pleasure of you feeling me." He'd brought a black satchel back from wherever he'd gone, which he set down as carefully as a carton of eggs. "Fact is, I don't believe Doc had the pleasure, either." He snorted in mirth. "Something evil, you said. You got that right. I'm ba-ad."

Charlie and Ross exchanged concerned glances. She was extremely thankful their lovemaking had been aborted. The idea of lying naked with Ross, under Cid's voyeuristic surveillance made her skin crawl.

Cid contemplated the sky, which had gone from gray to purest blue. "After I saw you fogies weren't going to do anything but sleep, I went on up to the second lake and did an equipment check. And fed the fish some pineapple." He sniffed and took a self-important stance, hands heeled into his hips. "I bet I exterminated every damn fish in that lake. Blew them right out of the water."

Cautiously, Ross said, "You had hand grenades?"

"Yeah. Didn't you hear them?"

They shook their heads.

Cid caught Ross's glance at the carry case and sneered, "Not in there. That's the sensitive stuff. Camera. Communications devices. I got a thousand dollars' worth of electronics in there." He drew himself straight, awaiting their admiration.

"How long have you been up here?"

"Same as you. I followed you guys, but you poked along so slow, I had to be careful not to run over you. Picnic lunches and kissy-face rest stops. When you went over to the creek, I climbed on past." He blew into his fists as if they were cold. "But I've been tailing you for days. Since Saturday night. I'm training myself for the CIA."

Ross swiped his bound hands through his hair and clutched the back of his head, trying to get his bearings. "Why follow me—us?" he asked.

"First it was just a training exercise. But soon as I heard the word *treasure*, it was a whole different thing."

"And when was that?" Ross persisted.

"I told you. Saturday night. You and the fortune teller there, were arguing about it in the van." He preened.

"You thought I was trying to take something out, and all the time I was putting something *in*. Think about it while I decide how to sift the lake."

Ross's bafflement was curdling into anger. Charlie watched, alarmed, as his face darkened, his eyes glittered, his mouth toughened in a thin line. "Cid," he began, low and dangerous.

"Cid, aren't you hungry?" Charlie cut in, like a sidekick drawing fire. "Let me make us something. Coffee, at least."

He fixed her with a glassy stare for several seconds. Then he strode over to Ross's meager stack of kitchenware, snatched up the coffeepot, and held it aloft as if it were a trophy to be admired. Taking a two-hop leadoff, he pitched it into the trees on the downhill side. It clanked twice on the descent.

Everyone thought hard for a while.

Cid began to pace beside the dead fire, picking up their belongings randomly to examine and discard. He found an apple, polished it against his chest, and bit out one side.

"May I make a suggestion?" Ross asked casually.

Cid shrugged.

"I've got some diving equipment in the van. Nothing fancy. Snorkel type."

Cid gnawed the apple core like corn on the cob before hurling it after the coffeepot. "Let me guess," he said. "I'm supposed to let Charlie go get it."

"Seems reasonable to me." Ross's lips imitated a smile.

Exploring his five o'clock shadow with the palm of one hand, Cid came to a decision. He grasped Charlie's arms and dragged her a couple of yards away from Ross, then stooped in front of her to untie her feet.

Charlie cautiously mimed hitting his exposed neck with her trussed hands, karate style, but Ross frowned a veto, knowing all she'd accomplish would be to infuriate Cid.

Tossing the bindings aside, Cid said, "Let's take a stroll, babe. And you—" He swung toward Ross. "You better be right here when we get back or it's goodbye, Charlie."

This wasn't what Ross had planned. "Take me, instead. She's a greenhorn hiking uphill. I can cut your time in half."

Not dignifying this with an answer, Cid told Charlie, "We got to secure our prisoner better. Get the adhesive tape out of the first-aid kit. I want you to wrap about ten layers around his wrists and ten around his ankles. Good and tight."

Even if her own wrists hadn't been tied, Charlie would have been awkward in her reluctance to enslave Ross further. As she wound tape over the straps on his wrists, his fingers stretched to brush hers in an oddly reassuring caress.

Cid noticed. "Wrap that tape around his fingers, too. Like a mummy, so he can't work himself loose."

When she'd done it to his satisfaction, Cid hauled her up. "Let's go."

"Want the van key?" Ross growled.

"Nah. I'll just break a window." His hand under Charlie's elbow lifted her shoulder toward her ear. "Pretty day," he noted, as if this were a social promenade.

"You better take a canteen," Ross called.

Cid didn't break stride or answer. They came to the top of the path, and Charlie briefly shut her eyes, imagining the return trip up its steepness with unsympathetic Cid and her hands tied. He gave her arm a little shake to start her down.

AS SOON AS they were out of sight, Ross began worrying the edges of the cloth tape with his teeth. Charlie had wrapped it as loosely as she dared, but when Cid checked it, he'd pressed and smoothed it and forced the free end down between Ross's wrists. Tasting glue and hearing the seconds click relentlessly on his watch, Ross looked out the corners of his eyes for something near and sharp to saw the tape against.

CHARLIE SLITHERED ahead of Cid down the trail, planning how to best protect herself when, inevitably, she fell. Arms up, hands on her scalp, the oversize coat sleeves protecting her face. Curl up but stay loose. Keep a stiff upper lip, she added for irony. Her mouth was dry already.

They came to a dogleg through boulders where the path went left and Charlie's momentum carried her right. Cid's hand grappled with the waistband of her jeans and swung her sideways, back on track. Eager to be free of his touch, she speeded up when she should have slowed down. Five thudding steps, and she threw up her arms for the fall. Expecting pain, she felt instead two steadying hands grasp her elbows from below, and parted them to peek through at Evan.

Astonished to see him, she gushed, "Boy, am I glad you were there. You may have saved my life."

His face, pink and perspiring from the climb, registered shock. Charlie looked down at herself and realized it was her tied wrists that horrified him. "Where's Ross?" he stammered.

"Up there." She motioned with her head. "Literally tied up."

Evan squeezed his temples between his fists and doubled over as if in mental pain. "Its all my fault. I should have told him about Cid's crazy ideas."

"I'm trying to think, here," Cid snarled.

The sudden silence was absolute, every breath held. Charlie could see that Evan was as apprehensive of what Cid would come up with as she was.

"Okay, troops, change of plan," was the decision. "Evan can go get the snorkel stuff from the van. But first come up to the camp. I've got something to give you."

Evan nodded, opened his mouth.

Somewhere above them, a huge snap of sound froze all three in attitudes of rapt attention.

After a moment of listening, Cid said, "What the hell was that?"

Evan spread his arms and shrugged. Charlie shook her head.

"Come on." Cid spun her around and shoved her uphill. "That mushhead better be right where we left him."

To avoid Cid's prodding fingers, Charlie swarmed up the path mostly on all fours, taking advantage of every root, bush or rock that offered a hold along the way. Chest heaving, thankful the distance wasn't greater, she stumbled into the homestead meadow, just ahead of Cid and Evan.

Ross looked up from studying the ground between his boots. His blandly innocent expression told Charlie he'd been working at freeing himself.

"Did you hear anything funny?" Cid demanded.

"Not in the last, oh, twelve hours," Ross said, wedging his wrists between his knees and flexing his arm muscles as if to stretch. Charlie hoped it was to hide the loosened bonds.

"What was that explosion, or whatever it was?" Cid eyed the camp for something out of place.

"A jet breaking the sound barrier? Hello, Evan. Somehow I'm not terribly surprised to see you."

"None of this was my idea. Mine's the sin of omission. I should have told you about Cid. You don't know how sorry I am."

Cid had turned his attention to opening the black satchel and taking out a pair of field radios. "Evan. I'm going to call you every ten minutes on this." He handed one over. "You've got an hour to go down to the van and back. If you don't answer me every time I page—" Cid narrowed his eyes and swept them toward Charlie "—someone's going to be sorry."

Evan nodded. "What is it I'm supposed to get?"

"Snorkel gear," Ross said. "It's in a red plastic box somewhere near the left wheel well."

Licking his lips, Evan put out a palm. "Keys?"

Ross rolled sideways on one hip. "Back pocket, Charlie."

The snugness of his jeans made it a tussle, getting the keys out. While her shoulder screened his mouth, he whispered, "Keep him occupied," which she took to mean Ross was working himself free.

Accepting the keys, Evan said, "Don't worry, guys. I'll be back."

It hadn't crossed Charlie's mind that Evan might not come back. Apparently it had crossed his. He scooped up her canteen, chugalugged it dry, and wiped his chin with his sleeve. Almost the old Evan again, he stuffed the radio into the front of his jeans, gave a two-fingered salute and stalked off.

Sinking down quietly beside Ross, Charlie tucked her feet under her, in hopes Cid would forget to retie them.

Cid ripped off his cap, scratched his head, flexed his shoulders, rolled his head a couple of times and shuffled away from them, aimlessly at first, then more purposefully around the corner of the cabin.

"That man will be a nervous wreck after an hour of waiting," Charlie whispered.

Ross put his face near her ear. "I don't care much for doing nothing myself." Her hair tickled his nose into a sneeze.

"Did you get loose?"

"My hands are. I used my teeth. I couldn't figure how to untie my feet without it showing—the straps would fall off."

"So what kind of escape plan can we come up with using your hands and my feet?"

"I say we lie low and pick the moment carefully. Anything we do is going to irritate Cid. We better be sure whatever move we make definitely puts us in charge."

"If he was really awake most of the night, maybe he'll doze off if we pretend to sleep ourselves."

"Good idea."

"Do you think Evan—" A shower of dirt pelted her head.

Cid, walking toward them, guffawed as they shook out their hair and collars. He scraped up a second handful of dry red soil and feinted an overhand throw before letting it sift between his fingers.

Approaching Charlie, he gripped his stomach and bowed. "May I have this dance?"

"Why don't you sit down and tell me about yourself."

"Oh, right, you're a shrink. You want to hear all about my slut mother and lush father and gross-out childhood. You can forget it. I did."

"I don't want to pry. It's just that conversation would make the time go faster."

Cid kicked her empty backpack over for a cushion and sat, his thin legs folding double with a popping of joints. "Okay, we'll talk, but I pick the subject."

Ross scooted into a prone position, only his head on the sleeping bag, and shut his eyes.

Cid said, "You're sure it's in the lake?"

"Yes."

"You know whereabouts in the lake?"

"Probably. I know where I'd try first."

"But you can't say what it is."

"No. I haven't been able to see that."

Cid stared at her. "Jeez, you give me the willies."

She wanted to tell him the feeling was mutual.

"How do you do it? Can you ask yourself what's going to happen and get a vision, or what?"

"I'm usually not able to predict the future. I take psychic readings off objects, people, the environment, that help me tune in to the past."

"Yeah, but you predicted me. You kept bleating last night how something bad was going to happen."

Charlie shook her head. "You were already here. I could fee—sense you from your past and present activities, not from what you'd do next."

"Uh-huh." He had sat still for an entire minute. His foot shot out to worry a pebble from the ground, and he began to build a pyramid. "How long you been able to read minds?"

"I don't read minds," she explained patiently. "My mind experiences a different time and place when I—"

"Come on, I bet you can read my mind. What am I thinking?" Cid fixed his gaze on Charlie's front and slowly dragged his tongue around his lips.

Charlie looked away, feeling blood tingle her cheeks.

"Right!" Cid roared, slapping his thigh.

He bounded to his feet, palmed the little stack of pebbles, and began lobbing them one by one at the cabin. Glancing down at Ross, Charlie saw a muscle in his jaw leap with every whack.

"You're major league material," Ross said in a deceptively mild voice.

"I've got the arm for it. But there's too much politics in sports. Wheeling-dealing. Stupid rules. Too many cowboys and mama's boys. That's why I got interested in intelligence. With covert operations, you live by your own wits."

During this disjointed litany, his store of missiles ran out. He put his hands into his pockets and pulled out Ross's knife to examine. "Stand over by that tree, Charlie, and I'll show you my knife-throwing act."

"No, thank you." She forced a smile, hoping he was kidding.

Ross rolled over to his side. "I'm going to take a nap."

"Ross," Charlie hissed, playing her part.

"I didn't sleep well last night. Sardines must be insomniacs."

"Ross!"

"You should sleep, too. It'll make the wait shorter."

"I'll rest, but I couldn't possibly sleep," she said, curling herself to fit the top of the other sleeping bag.

"Let's see how our good buddy's doing," Cid said, picking up the radio and extending the antenna in two strokes. "Evan, give us a shout, here."

Charlie's stomach growled, and the answering voice on the radio sounded remarkably similar. She slid her eyes shut as Cid patrolled restlessly. She heard him kick at the dead fire and smelled ashes. He stopped beside her and nudged her knee.

"If your specialty's the past, why don't you look back a half hour and tell me what that loud noise was."

"Mmm," she answered.

"Say, Charlie, there's a big spider on your sleeve." Cid's sly voice reminded her of all the male practical jokers she'd encountered from kindergarten through high school.

She wouldn't give him the attention he craved. She didn't move a muscle, not even when he stirred the hair over her ear with what felt like a branch of tumbleweed.

7

SHE CAME AROUND with the stricken sensation of having
overslept. Her watch indicated at least twenty minutes
had elapsed. Ross's tousled head lay inches from hers,
and his even breathing suggested he, too, had actually
fallen asleep.

Cautiously she raised herself up to look for Cid.

"Right behind you, babe." His flat voice chilled her
with the suddenness of a snake's rattle.

He'd rebuilt the fire. It cracked and leaped. As she
blinked against the glare, he showed his beautiful teeth
and held aloft the next crumpled page before lowering it
into the flame.

"No!" she choked, tipping onto her hands and knees
and staggering up. He sidestepped her rush, holding the
journal at arm's length, enjoying her desperate attack.

"Hee, hee, hee. Can't get me," he taunted just before
she hit him in the throat with her tied fists.

He gagged and dropped the diary at the edge of the
fire. Charlie might have saved herself if she hadn't paused
to sweep the book out of jeopardy with her boot. Cid's
splayed fingers on the back of her head, his other hand
over her nose and mouth, formed a suffocating vice.
Fighting to get his own breath, he ignored her plight.

Ross's sleeping body did not so much as twitch. He was
too far away to kick. Her eyes blurred and her ears began to ring. From a great distance, Cid coughed. Just be-

fore she lost consciousness, his hand shook free of her hair, and she could bet he was reaching for his knife.

Ross had begun to dream of two bears fighting when one of them sprang at him and bit into his side. His eyes shot open as Cid's foot drew back for a second kick.

"Hey!" Ross rolled out of range, pressing his hands against his chest to hide the loose bonds. "Whatever happened to a gentle shake of the shoulder?"

"You got any rope in the van, case we have to haul something off the lake bottom?" Cid demanded.

Mouth open to answer affirmatively, Ross squinted at a patch of blue on the other side of the camp fire, and, recognizing what it was, he squirmed to a sitting position, heart pounding. "What's wrong with Charlie?"

Cid shrugged elaborately, not interested.

"Untie my feet so I can go help her."

Fingering his chin, Cid said, "It's maybe too late for that."

Ross lunged, forgetting his useless feet, and pitched forward on his face, just short of the smoldering fire. Tasting ashes, blinking dust, he shoved up to a kneeling position. If Cid had been watching, he'd have seen the straps drop from Ross's wrists. But Cid was loping back toward Charlie.

Ross swung his feet to the front and picked frantically at the adhesive tape. It ripped away exposing the lumpy knot of the backpack straps. He tried to untie it to no avail. As he was casting about for something sharp, he kicked into the fire and raked out a white branch. Tossing the cooler end from hand to hand, he rested the hot brand against the rayon bindings. They shriveled and melted; he wrenched his feet apart and staggered up wiping his eyes with a sleeve.

Cid was on one knee by Charlie, knife imbedded in the ground beside his foot. Lost in contemplations of his own he wasn't aware of Ross, and certainly didn't hear him pounding across the meadow. Punting the knife toward the trees, Ross followed through with a flying tackle on Cid's bent back. They crashed into unforgiving rock, both grunting with pain. Arm locked on Cid's neck, Ross levered with the strength of fright and anger.

Cid stabbed backward with his elbows, clawed at Ross's hair and eyes, and, still losing, choked, "Give. I give."

"No tricks!"

"No. I quit!" Cid gurgled.

Ross forced him over, facedown in the dirt, before loosening the hold and backing on to his feet. "Clasp your hands behind your head and don't move."

Cid complied, slowly and with colorful commentary. Ross turned out Cid's pockets to reclaim the money and pocketknife Cid had confiscated earlier, and he tucked the radio into his own waistband.

Circling to Charlie's far side to keep Cid in view, Ross knelt and touched her smooth throat. The cadence of her heart telegraphed against his fingers. Frowning, he carefully turned her unbruised face and massaged her skull. No lumps. No blood. He exhaled at last, wondering if modern woman knew how to swoon.

Patiently, he worked at the knots securing her hands. When they gave way, he rearranged Charlie with her head on the jacket, and took off his own to cover her.

Glaring at Cid, he growled, "I'm going to ask you one more time, scumbrain. What's wrong with Charlie?"

A hoarse answer came from beside his foot. "Her mouth's too wide, and she's psychic," Charlie said, obviously grateful for being back amongst the living.

Ross grinned at her. "I don't think your mouth's too wide."

"Ha," she said weakly. "You also don't think I'm psychic."

Keeping a vigilant eye on Cid, Ross leaned over Charlie and lowered his voice. "What happened?"

She wiped her mouth with the back of one hand. "He was burning your grandmother's journal, so I jumped him, and he tried to smother me. High altitude is tough enough. This was like *no* altitude." She smiled reassurance.

"You have a dirty face," he said, wanting to kiss the smudges anyway.

She coughed up a laugh. "Yours is filthy. What's that gray stuff?"

"Ashes. Want to wash up?"

She nodded and pushed to a sitting position.

Ross steadied her with a hand on her shoulder. "I'll incapacitate Attila over there, and we'll go get some water."

"Hands in back," Charlie cautioned, offering him his jacket and reaching for her own.

"I'd like to wrap his arms around twice before tying." Ross gathered up the straps that he'd taken off Charlie's wrists and approached Cid warily.

There was a short scuffle when Cid halfheartedly made his last stand. But Ross had little difficulty jamming a knee into Cid's back, forcing his arms behind him, tying his wrists and ankles. Hoisting him upright, Ross towed him across the meadow to the sleeping bags. When Charlie approached, Cid's epithets converted to feminine gender.

"Give it a rest," Ross snapped, and, to everyone's surprise, Cid did.

Charlie searched the ground for the journal she'd saved. Like a wounded animal, it sprawled open on its spine. She scooped it up and tucked it inside her shirt.

Snatching up a canteen, Ross hugged Charlie to him as they walked toward the creek. He wanted to burst into song or turn cartwheels to express his immense relief that she was safe.

Instead, he squeezed her and said, "One more time. You sure you're okay?"

"Umpf! Unless you just broke one of my ribs."

At the creek, Ross filled the canteen. He dampened his white handkerchief for a washcloth, gallantly using it on Charlie first. As the cold water touched her cheek, she flinched, then held absolutely still. Ross bent to rinse and wring the cloth; he dabbed her forehead, swiped across her nose, circled her eyes.

He was about to kiss her, never mind his dirty face, when she sighed, "No."

He pulled back to see her eyes. Their fixed, glassy stare sent a shiver skipping down his backbone. "Charlie?"

She didn't seem to hear or see him.

Ross's hands, no longer gentle, clasped her shoulders. "Not now, damn it, Charlie. I'm sick of your fat, white lady. Look at me." He jiggled her, trying, unsuccessfully, to break the spell, feeling his own eyes widen as hers became enormous. "What do you see, Charlie?" he fairly shouted.

She blinked and looked, really looked, at him. "Oh, Ross," she breathed. "The dam is breaking."

He opened his mouth to say something cruel, and then he froze, listening to an echoing crack similar to the one they'd heard earlier that morning. A high breeze whipped the treetops without stirring the ground and died with the abruptness of a thrown switch. Into the hush, far in the distance, a keening whine began to intensify into a howl. Ross looked down, horrified, at the sparkling creek prancing at his feet.

Charlie fumbled to take his hand. "Come on, we've got to do what the signs say—climb to higher ground." She pulled at him.

"This way!" He strong-armed her the opposite direction. "Around the creek. There's a path to a mesa that'll be safe."

"No! Cid!" she reminded him, breaking his grasp and starting to run.

Ross followed hard on her heels, passing her after they gained the clearing. Sprinting across the field, he glanced at the serene cabin and brooding cliff wall supporting Sayers Lake, and he pictured Chokecherry Lake, unchecked and rampant, on its way to savage this idyllic spot. Wanting to scream, he grabbed Cid's ankles and began to chop at the straps.

"You know what that noise is?" Ross panted. "There's a flood on the way. I'm cutting you loose and you're on your own." The rayon parted and Ross leaped up to cut free Cid's hands. "Follow us if you want. But if you don't behave yourself, I'm going to shove you over a cliff."

Not waiting for an answer, he tossed aside the straps and whirled to hustle Charlie back the way they'd come. As he clutched her elbow, the radio against his back began to spit faint words.

"Cid . . . at the van . . . the gear . . ."

"Oh, God, Evan." Ross swept the radio up to his mouth. "Evan! It's Ross. Chokecherry Dam is breaking. Repeat, the dam is breaking. Evan, you've got to warn the people down canyon. There's a bullhorn behind the van passenger seat. Read me?"

The radio burped static as Charlie and Ross stared at each other. Cid was doing a dance of impatience, trying to decide which direction to run.

Ross held the radio out to him. "Am I doing this right? Tell him the dam's going."

Cid's eyes rolled like those of a panic-stricken horse. "Let's get out of here!" he bellowed.

"Close enough," Ross muttered. "Evan, people are going to die if you don't warn them. Move it!"

Not waiting for confirmation, he grabbed Charlie's hand and they raced toward the creek. The flood's voice had increased to a jet engine roar. Choke Creek continued to tumble innocently along its shallow bed.

"Step where I step," Ross told Charlie, and he led her across on flat stones while Cid splashed through the water and reached the steeply angled path first.

The steady crash of the approaching flood beat against their ears, a continuous, distracting roar. It was horrible to be climbing toward the noise when every instinct demanded they run the opposite direction. Once, disoriented, Charlie took three steps downhill before Ross caught and turned her around.

She gulped mouthfuls of dusty, metallic-smelling air, willing her legs to hoist her up one more foot of altitude, and then one more, and one more again. A red squirrel in full flight the wrong way scampered between their feet.

Charlie tripped, her foot too leaden to clear a bump of dirt-covered root. She seriously considered resting, cheek against the rubble, legs luxuriously slack, but Ross pried her up and dragged her another five yards to the brow of the mesa where they collapsed, panting, in the rabbitbrush.

When her head stopped spinning, Charlie raised it to find their refuge was a stony mountaintop with views falling away on every side, taller mountains ringing it. Ross had gone to the edge to look into the valley they'd escaped. Charlie weaved her way in that direction as if drunk, avoiding Cid, who sat, knees drawn up, face hidden in his arms. As she reached the drop-off and Ross put out a cautioning hand, she sank to her knees and craned to see the bottom.

Little Choke Creek ran muddy brown, its boundaries wider. Dark water, thick as cement, oozed into every cranny of the ravine.

From this vantage point, they could see, like the three rings of a circus, three levels of terrain. Lowest, on their right, the Sayers homestead lay deserted of all but their scattered belongings. Only a front portion of the cabin roof showed, the rest shielded by the cliff overhang.

Straight across but below their elevation, Sayers Lake glittered in the morning light.

And to their left, at about their altitude, what had been a placid wilderness reservoir, Chokecherry Lake, was boiling over its banks and smashing down the mountainside.

Ross pointed to an area between the upper and lower lakes where a stately ponderosa pine sailed, limbs, needles and bark, above the other trees. Another tree exploded, the javelin top spinning away. Like dominoes, all the evergreens began to topple, shrieking as they fell.

What remained of the dam wall was crumbling away in great chunks; it seemed to dissolve before their eyes. The pent-up water, a released beast, reared up and rushed away. Boulders ran with it. Huge fists of rock spilled down the slope, splashing gouts of water. The strange, hot odor, Charlie realized, was granite grinding against granite.

Chokecherry Lake cascaded the mile toward Sayers Lake, which lay like a giant speed bump across the flood's path to the valley. Much of the water continued to detour into Choke Creek, transforming it into a chaotic river, but Chokecherry was gorging the smaller lake. They could see the waterline rocking on Sayers Dam rise with every lap, like a bathtub about to overflow.

And the bathtub that was Chokecherry Lake was nearly drained dry. As its watery ammunition ran out, the destruction tapered off and the decibel level gradually decreased. Ross could put his mouth near Charlie's ear and yell encouragement.

Sayers Lake continued to rise. They watched it come level with the top of the dam and begin to slop over the sides. Except for the sound of fast-running water, the mesa quieted.

Charlie gritted her teeth against the chill spasms of shock and managed to ask, "What happens next?"

"It won't hold. Sayers Dam can't contain that much extra water. It may spill over the sides for a while, but pretty soon it'll punch right through. And then it has a straight shot down the canyon to the road and on down to the outskirts of Boulder. Let's hope Evan found the bullhorn."

Ross noticed he was still clutching the radio. He stretched out the antenna and stabbed buttons. "Evan. Evan," he called and listened. "I hope he's too far away."

"That first cracking noise we heard this morning while Cid and I were on the trail—" Charlie thought out loud.

"It must have been the dam beginning to let go," Ross said. "It apparently sealed itself again, delaying the complete breach for a while."

The flood could have come then, while Ross was alone and tied up in the meadow, and Cid would have left him to die.

"If you don't stop shimmying around, you're going to fly apart," Ross said, drawing her to his chest and bundling his jacket around them both.

His tenderness made Charlie's eyes sting. She slid her arms up his back and hung on fiercely. Ross murmured endearments meant to soothe, but they made her want to cry all the more.

"Tell me about the dam," she said to distract them both. "When it was built and how and stuff like that."

Ross glanced at Cid, still hunched in an attitude of despondency. "Let's see. Both the lakes were man-made around 1900. Well, take that back. Chokecherry was already here, a natural lake, and they just dammed up the lower end."

"Who's they?"

"Ditch company. There are hundreds of little mountain reservoirs like these that supply water for flatland irrigation."

"What would make the dam burst?" Charlie prompted.

"Old age. Aggravated, no doubt, by Cid's demolition orgy in the wee hours. These old dams are made of piled rock in a concrete skin. After eighty years of holding back thousands of tons of water, they tend to get tired." He smiled down at her forehead and brushed it with his lips.

"Your grandparents were living here when Sayers Lake was dammed up. So the treasure could be in the ground under the lake," she deduced sadly. "Or if your grandfather put it into the lake water, it might be washed away with the flood today. Either way, you may not find it."

"Afraid so," Ross agreed.

"You don't sound very upset about it."

"I can't miss what I never had," he answered reasonably.

The words echoed in her mind, triggering a pang of regret. Oh, but I'll miss you, Ross Davies, she thought. I'll miss *you*.

She cringed as a sharp report reverberated across the canyon. Sayers Dam was about to breach. Water had been steadily overflowing the sides of the lake, converting trail to stream, cliff to meager waterfall that drummed the cabin roof. But now from right to left, the top of the dam peeled away, loosing a clot of dirt, rock and water. Another section of dam belched free, and the cliff became a mini Niagara, completely engulfing the cabin.

As the dam wall disappeared, the noise level increased. Charlie covered her ears, wanting to cover her eyes as well when she saw splintered planks beginning to float from under the cliff. The dam, in complete rout now, crumbled flush with the rock cliff, and Sayers Lake poured free.

Ross was finding it strangely exciting to sit in this front row center seat overlooking a catastrophe in progress while Charlie's soft curves fit warmly against his body. He felt guilty about it. There might be people fighting—and losing—a battle with the water cannonballing down the canyon. But there was nothing more he could do except wait for the helicopters that would eventually come to examine the scene of the disaster.

He was hungry, for food as well as for Charlie. With a quick glance at Cid, who was sitting with hands clamped to his ears, Ross rooted under Charlie's jacket and shirt to stroke her bare back.

Gazing absently at Sayers Lake, he thought about building a fire so they could warm up and summon rescuers at the same time. As he calculated how long it might be before someone would come for them, part of Ross's mind noted that the lake was about two-thirds gone, and its topography was becoming prominent. Jagged rocks lined the steep, inner sides, and a corrugated outlet pipe, big enough for a man to crawl through, protruded from the far bank.

Depending on how soon Evan could tell the authorities about them, rescue might be as soon as this afternoon. Ross wanted to check his watch, but it was on the arm that currently swaddled Charlie's delectable back.

His eyes suddenly focused on what they'd failed to register during his daydream. A boulder in the center of the lake bed was, because of the receding water, rising up. Unlike the surrounding red sandstone, it was pale, almost white. And out of it, like a crocodile scouting his territory, two great eyes met Ross's startled regard. The water lapped lower, gradually exposing the long straight nose, and lower, the gently curving upper lip.

Charlie felt Ross's throat rumble an exclamation. She tilted her head to see his expression, then followed the direction of his stare.

The familiar face—domed forehead to squared-off chin—grew out of the lake. Predating Mount Rushmore by some forty years, Grandfather Sayers's carving of George Washington gazed serenely at the Colorado landscape.

Charlie's eyes sparkled as she turned to mouth, *"Beautiful!"*

They watched his neck emerge. The graceful tail of a granite ribbon curled along one side. The water sucked lower, revealing row on row of ruffled jabot.

A thought swiveled Charlie toward Ross again. "That's the white lady!" she shouted, pleased with herself.

Ross threw back his head and laughed.

The flood was suspenseful in a new way now. What would be disclosed next? Was Washington full figure? The top button of a vest made that seem possible. Charlie wished she had a pair of binoculars as she strained to locate other sculptures. She especially looked for the animals she'd envisioned.

But the water emptied out, and nothing more came into view. The din began to lessen, like a thunderstorm passing on. Charlie relaxed against Ross's broad chest.

She thought of his father, fishing at the edge of the lake, somehow catching sight of the monolithic face, leaping up, and off balance, falling into the icy water. Drowning. Perhaps it was his death she'd identified with, making the huge white "lady" vaguely ominous.

Ross reluctantly separated himself from Charlie. "I've gotta go. Work to do."

"Can I help?"

"We need some dry wood to make a fire." He offered her a hand up. "You don't happen to have a candy bar on you, do you?"

"You think I'm an idiot?" she said, softly imitating Cid's snarl. "I'm not giving you any chocolate to throw in my face."

Ross grinned and dropped an arm over her shoulders, drawing her with him toward a scrawny stand of evergreens he had spotted earlier on as a possible source of kindling.

"Ross," she said, stooping to admire a fuzzy alpine flower. "Are you ready to admit I'm psychic?"

He didn't answer immediately, which warned her, and when he did answer, it was with a question. "Where are the animals?"

"I don't know," she snapped. "Maybe we'd see them if we were closer to the lake," she added more sociably.

Ross used his heel on a piece of tree stump, gathered up the fragments and deposited them in Charlie's arms, chucking her under the chin. "I'm not sure you get any points for Washington, either. Your reception must have been pretty badly garbled to mistake the father of our country for an overweight woman."

"That's exactly how it works sometimes, but it's the *per*ception not the reception that's faulty. I just didn't recognize what I was seeing."

Giving her a condescending smile that made her consider dropping the wood on his feet, Ross said, "Does that mean the animals are going to turn out to be the first presidential cabinet?"

She showed him her teeth, but it wasn't a smile. "If you knew anything about parapsychology, you'd know that revelations are not always literal. Like in your dreams. You may dream about a snake. But it isn't really a snake, it's some person you don't trust. In my vision, animals might have represented—" She paused only a second. "Noah! The ark. A flood!"

"You don't do futures, remember?"

"Not this flood. The one that filled up the lake when the dam was built. That covered Grandfather Sayers's Washington."

He grunted noncommittally and turned away.

Angry, she picked out a safer target. "How could they do that?" she blurted. "How could they be so callous?"

"Who?" He'd found another stump that would require a more sophisticated tool than his boot.

"The dam builders. The damned dam builders. They just threw up their wall and went on their merry way and didn't care that a masterpiece was being buried under tons of water."

"They probably couldn't do anything else. The land Grandfather found his raw material on was government property. And how many art lovers would ever trek up here to view the sculpture? That irrigation water was going to be a lot more valuable to a lot more people than the giant likeness of a president."

She tossed her head and jutted her jaw. "It could have been moved. The government could have moved it."

Ross studied her lovely, stubborn profile. "There must not have been anyone around like you at the time—a crusader who'd have done the necessary prodding and bushbeating to get the job done."

Unsure if this was criticism or compliment, Charlie continued to glare into the distance. The afternoon sun rolled cloud shadows across the mountains. She jumped when Ross touched her arm.

"My grandfather would have liked you. I like you. One hell of a lot."

Cupping the back of her head with his hands, he kissed her. The warmth of his mouth softened her set lips, melted her anger, and seeped right into her bones. She pushed against him, oblivious to the sharp-angled stump wood crushed between them. As he licked the corners of her mouth, Charlie grinned a Mona Lisa smile, which he covered with a harsher kiss. She matched him, desire for desire, her mouth open and welcoming. They broke apart and joined again, each feeding on the other's hunger.

Charlie wanted to throw aside the wood, strip away her clothes, and sink to the ground holding Ross. She wanted him to kiss her everywhere, the same way he now tormented her mouth. She trembled and ached, and her throat swelled around a silent, begging cry.

As Ross opened passion-glazed eyes, Cid's rangy silhouette crossed his peripheral vision. Groaning, with superhuman effort, he put Charlie at arm's length.

"Rain check?" Ross said in a hoarse whisper. He inclined his head in Cid's direction.

Charlie nodded, embarrassed by her runaway sexuality, and knelt to retrieve the wood that had escaped her grip. To hide the unsteadiness of his legs, Ross stamped away, trying to renew his interest in collecting firewood. Charlie carried her arm load to a blackened hollow near the trailhead and let it thump to the ground. Cid was standing at the cliff edge watching the subsiding flood.

"You can see the treasure now," Charlie called vindictively. "I think you'll need help getting it down the mountain."

He raised a hand to gesture contempt before striding to the path and slip-sliding out of sight.

Ross had disappeared down the other side of the mesa. For want of something better to do, Charlie arranged and rearranged the wood, trying to make it look like a camp fire, till he returned, puffing from exertion. He carelessly dumped his load of logs on top of her handiwork, and asked, "Where's Cid?"

"Down the trail. He left about ten minutes ago."

"Dumb kid probably expects to walk to the road—in hip-high, muddy water—through a scoured-out creek bottom full of boulders."

They listened to the distant thundering of the departed flood. Then Ross shook himself and went for more wood, and Charlie wandered to the overlook to admire, again, the Washington head.

The sun's angle had changed, painting shadows beside the nose, under the forehead and chin. She could see, now, that the work was unfinished. Although the likeness was instantaneously recognizable as that of George Washington, the features had not been planed and perfected. The shoulders and chest emerged from raw, irregular stone. It was primitive and powerful art.

How long, Charlie wondered, had it taken Timothy to bring the statue this far out of its granite shell? How did he feel when the lake buried it? Did he realize how fine a carving he'd made?

A foot tumbled pebbles behind her, and she turned to smile welcome, but it was Cid she saw. Mud caked his jeans, the state of his jacket indicated he'd fallen on his back, the stocking cap was missing and mud splotched his stringy hair.

And his mood had not improved with the experience. The look he threw Charlie froze her in place. He slouched to the campsite and sat down, and Charlie crossed the mesa in search of more congenial company.

Ross came staggering into view balancing a hefty branch on each shoulder. "Ugh. Caveman's mate meets him at end of hard day. This is good."

Charlie put her finger to her lips and motioned with her head. "He's back and he's not smiling," she whispered. "Be careful what you say."

Ross made a "Who me?" gesture and led her back to camp. It took four matches to start the fire. With the air of a maître d', Ross guided Charlie to a flat rock several feet from the fire, seated her on it, and sat himself on the bare dirt with his back between her legs, arms draped over her knees. Across the fire, Cid's face undulated like the mirror in Snow White.

Charlie hastily dropped her gaze to the top of Ross's unruly blond head, bent forward and rested her cheek on it. He patted her shin in acknowledgement.

The afternoon trickled by. Ross tended the fire, stretched, studied the valley, and listened for a helicopter. Charlie watched him, memorizing his features and the way he moved, foreseeing how lonely it would be back in Chicago.

Cid glowered at the fire, immobile as a carnivore with its prey in sight. Once he startled them, announcing, "That bag was worth a thousand bucks."

"It was worth more than that," Ross said. "Your radios may have saved a lot of lives."

"The camera alone cost a couple hundred," Cid whined, missing the point.

The sun set early behind the serrated horizon. Stars began to show. Now and then an airplane winked across the sky. A chill breeze sliced through the open mesa, and Ross traded places with Charlie to put her in the protective circle of his arms.

"Ever heard of Alferd Packer?" he lipped against her ear.

The shaking of her head degenerated into shaking in general.

Ross squeezed her so hard she couldn't shiver. "He was stranded in a blizzard on a mountain pass, and to avoid starving, he turned cannibal."

Charlie expressed revulsion with one evocative syllable into her upturned coat collar.

"I'd like to eat you," Ross insinuated softly. "I'd like to taste your salty-sweet skin, and bite you just hard enough to almost hurt. Your stomach and your breasts and your shoulders and—other places."

She squirmed, glancing uneasily at Cid's intense face, while Ross continued to tease her, his voice the barest brush of sound beside her neck. "Charlie, we were too close to death today. Time's a-wasting. When we get off this mountain, when we get home, I can promise you—" She held her breath, her eyelids sliding down to black out all but the gentle buzz of words. "I'm going to take you into my bed. We're going to lie together, no one and nothing between us. And we're going to kiss and touch and drive each other crazy. Over and over."

She trembled, but she wasn't cold anymore. Opening her eyes, she met Cid's hostile gaze, and all her pleasure slipped away, like the water from Chokecherry Lake.

Grunting, Ross stood to feed the fire, which was showering sparks in the wind. "I'm going for another load of wood. If you need me, yell." He gave them each a meaningful look and tramped off.

"Is there anything you'd like to talk about, Cid?" she asked hesitantly, aware of tempting trouble.

"Leave me alone. You don't care about me. Nobody ever does."

Tartly she said, "Don't judge me by whoever misused you in the past. I sincerely want to try to ease your pain." And she inwardly winced, expecting a lewd wisecrack.

He surprised her with, "My name is really Louis. Louis Stillicidious."

She repeated it. "What an unusual name. I like the way it rolls off your tongue."

"You should've heard how some of my teachers pronounced it. They'd get it all wrong." He snorted. "One of them shortened it to Cid. He was an okay guy. I didn't mind."

Settling into a listening attitude, chin on fist, she waited for more. The fire shifted and fell in on itself. "I don't want to talk about my parents," he said without emotion after a while. Then he stretched out with his back to her, head on extended arm.

As Charlie was starting to fight sleep Ross returned and slid down beside her. "Is this the right line for the bus to Boulder?" he asked.

She exercised her cramped elbow. "Would a helicopter come up here at night?"

"Possibly, but probably not with this much wind." His jacket rustled as he wrapped an arm around Charlie and patted his thigh. "Put your head down and sleep if you want. We won't leave without you."

"I think I'm the one who should keep watch. Do you know how hard you are to wake up? There could be a full-scale war up here, and you'd outsnore it."

"I don't snore," Ross protested, bypassing the real issue. "But okay, we'll both watch."

He gave her fifteen minutes to fall asleep. It was closer to ten when her head drooped against his shoulder. He sat very still, as if her limp weight were precious glass.

8

ROUGH HANDS shook her awake. Charlie swallowed a protest, expecting to find Cid looming over her. But pale hair backlit by the fire identified Ross, hauling her to her feet.

"What's the matter?" she asked.

But he was gone, rushing to waken Cid. A rumble, like tires on a rickety bridge, made her hold her breath, confused. Weren't they high on a mesa, safe from floods and avalanches?

For one hanging second, the whole dome of night sky glowed white, and she felt the first drops of icy rain. Moments later, the rattle of thunder sounded, nearer than before.

His face blank with interrupted sleep, Cid swayed to his feet, and Ross strode back to take Charlie's arm and quickstep her to the trailhead. Lightning revealed the yawning descent.

"Now you get to see the other side of Colorado's weather," Ross said, leading off single file.

Shuffling her feet, testing the slope, Charlie heard Cid wheezing behind her. She shrank into her jacket as light and sound struck almost simultaneously; her scalp tingled with static as raw electricity dissipated in the wet air. Cid whimpered before pushing past her to slither down the path.

Ross flattened himself against a boulder to let Cid go by, yelling after him, "Find an overhang." He reached to drag Charlie deeper into the canyon, away from the lightning bolts threatening the high ground.

There weren't any overhangs. They slid down the trail to escape the lightning, but there was no escape from the rain. It came in sheets, as if it were an intelligence determined to wash them off the mountain. They skidded to the bottom and teetered on the edge of Choke Creek.

"Cid! Give me your arm. We'll make a chair for Charlie."

"No!" Charlie shouted. "Too awkward!" And she stepped into the thick water up to her knees, to end further argument.

Ross plunged in next to her and clutched the tail of her jacket. "Wait! Take my hand. Cid, hold hands!"

Charlie half turned in the other direction and stretched out an arm to Cid, still hesitating on the bank. With uncustomary docility, he clasped her hand in his callused, chilly hand and splashed determinedly forward.

The water was so cold and numbed their legs so quickly, Charlie had to look down to see if hers were actually moving. Their feet probed the slippery, ruptured creek bed; rocks twisted their ankles, potholes tripped them. Once Charlie's boots flew out from under her, dragging the men together as water rushed up to her rib cage. It didn't matter. She was already saturated, hair pasted to her face and neck, rain dripping from her nose and chin.

They reached a rise, a spit of land that must have been the creek's original border, where trees, single file, had divided it from the meadow. The three stood there, despondently scanning, whenever lightning flared, the sea of murky water.

"Where were you aiming?" Charlie shouted.

"Behind the cabin," Ross answered. "I mean behind where the cabin used to be," he corrected.

He tested the water in front of his boot. It came to his ankle. He tugged gently at Charlie's hand, and she followed, drawing along an unresisting Cid.

More rocks. More slippery mud and chuckholes. The deepest it got was up to Charlie's calves. She trudged doggedly across the seemingly endless floodplain, her mind, like her legs, beginning to numb. Air and rain gusted into her face. She could cry and no one would ever know. But it was too much effort to cry.

She stubbed her toe and looked down at a stony beach—the end of the water. Another few steps led to the cavelike depression of the cliff overhang. Shaking both hands free, she collapsed on the rock floor, her back to the wall. Cid fell down almost on top of her. She could hear his teeth clicking. Her own muscles ached from the shivering.

Ross knelt, fumbled a box into her hand, and closed her stiff fingers around it. "Guard that well. It's the matches."

He squeezed her knee as he stood up, and a trickle of water ran down her leg. She thought it was funny, but she couldn't seem to shape her mouth correctly for a laugh. A flash of lightning illuminating the area confirmed that Ross was gone. Charlie and Cid pressed together, everything forgotten except the agonizing craving for warmth.

Gradually the lightning stopped, the thunder mumbled off into the distance, and the rain turned to mist. Charlie began to feel warmer and thought of hypothermia—blood deserting her extremities, sluggishly pumping a shorter route around her body until her brain, starving for oxygen, shut down and let death in.

And shouldn't Ross be back? She screamed his name, but the prowling wind threw it back into her face. If she had to die, she wanted to be in his arms. Pinching her eyes shut, wishing they'd made love, she remembered what he'd said about the treasure: I can't miss what I've never had. But she did miss, horribly, the intimacy she'd never known with him.

Somewhere along the cliff, like a leaky faucet, the leftover rain performed a Chinese torture, drip, drip, dripping. A foot scuffed pebbles. Ross. In spite of legs as insensible as two balloons, Charlie leaped up to hug him. Whatever he was carrying he eased to the floor of the shelter.

His voice was hollow and tired. "We're in trouble, folks."

Charlie found his cold hand and wrapped it tightly inside both of hers.

"There's no dry material for a fire. All the kindling was either scoured away by the flood or soaked in the storm. If we could get out of these wet clothes, we'd have a chance, but there's nothing to wrap up in, so we're back to square one."

Cid's boot thumped something. "Don't you call that a log?"

"Yeah. One log. I found it hiding out in a niche in a boulder. It's dry, but it might as well be wringing wet because I don't have anything to get it started. Twigs, newspapers, nothing. You can't start a blaze with nothing but one log."

"At least try." Charlie slid the matches into his hand.

There were tiny noises as Ross handled the box, and then, "Ten," he said. "Ten matches."

He crouched down, back bowed protectively, and the first one chirred into flame. He held it to a splintered corner of the wood and, when the stub seared his fingers, carefully fitted it into the V between bark and core. A string of black smoke unwound several inches into the air and the tiny flame went out.

Ross tried again. The match blackened and shriveled like a fireworks snake and winked out. He felt his pockets, put the matches into his driest shirt pocket, and tore the box into strips. Laying them on the log, he ignited a third match and touched the cardboard. The miniature fire reflected in three pairs of hopeful eyes till it, too, died.

"Maybe if you put all the matches in at once," Charlie said.

"That would certainly bring a quick end to our suspense." Charlie heard the rasp of whiskers as he wiped his hand across his face. "I'd burn my money if it wasn't a sodden mess."

"I got a few bills," Cid said. "They don't feel too bad."

The paper exchanged hands in the dark, a match sizzled, and Charlie saw two crumpled fives and a one lick up the fire and scorch the log. Ross carefully fanned the flames, but they withered to nothing.

Ross's voice sighed out of the blackness, "Easy come, easy go." He snatched up the log and began smashing it on the ground.

"Ross!"

"It's okay. I'm breaking off the loose stuff for starter."

Charlie slumped at the wall, hurting in every joint. She lapped the damp jacket tighter and hugged herself hard. And felt something sharp-edged and solid dig into her ribs—the journal.

"We'll save one match and put the rest in one basket, like Charlie said, all or nothing," Ross announced. "I'm making a nest of splintered scraps that we'll add the matches to. Find me a couple of rocks to hold the log higher off the floor."

"Ross," Charlie breathed too low, then louder, "Ross."

"Right here," he answered, preoccupied.

She blundered into him, found his hand, and pushed his fingers around his grandmother's journal, only the cover damp, and warm from being tucked inside her shirt.

"Ha-cha-cha!" he rejoiced. "You win the MVP award."

"I may be most valuable, but this isn't play," Charlie complained, hope strengthening her voice. "Let's hurry up and have a little heat around here."

In the dark, each page was torn, wadded and stuffed under the log. Charlie winced every time a new page was ripped out and silently thanked Grandmother Sayers for having kept a diary.

"What are you doing?" Cid asked. When the match lighted, he studied the log in its antique paper bed, momentarily puzzled.

Ross fed the match the length of the log; each place he touched, the sepia paper caught into a fragile flame, drying and heating the log. He dropped the match end into a growing blaze and picked up the journal again.

Cid said, "How come it's okay if he does it, but when I tried to do that, you got mad?"

Charlie turned, startled, and saw that he was trying to smile at his joke, and she tried to smile, too.

The belly of the log began to smoke in earnest. "Come on, come on, 'atta girl," Ross crooned, stuffing another day of his grandmother's life into the pyre. He crumpled the next page ready for wherever it was needed. Scorched paper fluttered out of the fire and sailed up the cliff side. The log burned.

Ross stepped back and looked through the heat waves at Charlie. They shared wan but triumphant smiles. Cid's legs folded up, and he began to unlace his boots.

"Cid's got the right idea," Ross said. "Take off everything that's wet. God, I wish I had found another log, but maybe this'll last an hour or so till daylight. We can expect a helicopter anytime after that."

Charlie began to peel off her jeans, realized her boots must go first, and sat gingerly on the bare rock. Spreading their clothes to dry on the other side of the inadequate fire, leaving on only underwear, the three of them huddled, shoulder to shoulder, toasting their legs and arms, fronts warm, backs bearably cold.

Mercifully, the wind slackened to nothing, and the scudding clouds began to flash glimpses of moon. Ross stared at Charlie's long, bare legs and mentally cursed Cid for staring, too.

Maybe it would help take their minds off their misery to talk about something—anything. "Why was it you put a bug in my van Saturday night, Cid?"

He gave a weak imitation of his manic laugh. "Big mistake, huh? Look where it got me."

"You didn't know about the treasure when you broke into the van. *I* didn't even know yet that was Charlie's mission in coming to Colorado."

"I'd just got this new bug, and I was looking for a place to try it out. Evan was on the phone to McCoy, setting up your party, and he was on the phone to you, about this mystery woman flying in, and I figured that tailing you would be as promising as tailing anyone else. So then I tune in on you two talking treasure!"

"Where'd you put it? The bug."

"It's stuck up under the driver's seat. You'll have a hard time finding it, even knowing where. It's smaller than a collar button." Cid's voice strengthened as he warmed to his subject. "That's nothing. There's transmitters that'll go in a slit in the side of a playing card."

"Uh, if you don't mind my asking," Ross said, "how'd you get the money for the electronic gadgets?"

"I said my father was a lush. I didn't say he wasn't rich," Cid answered with surprising mildness.

They lapsed into a miserable silence that Ross broke with the suggestion that everyone get some sleep. No one slept. They kept a dumb, exhausted vigil, willing the log to last, watching it begin to whiten and fur with ashes. Ross rolled it over once and it burned brighter. He tore up the rest of the journal, nursing the heat with paper tidbits.

When he was down to one page, he smiled sadly at Charlie, ripped it out, and offered it to her. "A souvenir," he said.

The words leaped at her: *They buryed T's treasure this day.* She solemnly rolled the paper into a cylinder, and, holding it like a flower, watched the fire cool.

Lighter sky in the east told them that the sun had cleared the plains horizon, but it would be hours before it touched the meadow where Charlie had begun to shiver again. Cid, too, was shaking.

He reeled upright and lumbered aimlessly around the shelter. "When the hell is somebody going to get here? Where's the cavalry, huh?" Leaning toward the swampy meadow, he screamed "Help!" three times at the top of his lungs.

Ross stood and snatched up his jeans, gritting his teeth as he jammed his legs into them and yanked them over his hips. Remembering the clammy coldness of wet bathing suits, Charlie flinched in sympathy.

"I'll see if I overlooked any wood," he said.

Charlie got up, stiffness precluding grace. "I'll go with you."

Ross had his boots on and was viciously pulling the strings into place, as if they were to blame. "No. I'll make better time without you."

Remembering the fear she'd felt earlier when he was gone, Charlie continued to collect her unappealing wardrobe. "The exercise will keep me warm."

Anxiety boiled over and Ross roared, "Do push-ups!" He whirled away from her. "You'll get more exercise than you ever dreamed of if we have to walk out of here on our own."

She opened her mouth to say something she knew she'd regret, but Cid saved her from it with, "Shut up!" He stood with one hand cupped to his ear. "Listen."

Charlie's heart jerked. Not again. Not a new flood, a new storm. And then she heard it too—the clack-clack-clack of rotor blades.

Ross's scowl smoothed into eyes-shut relief. He twisted toward Charlie and they beamed at each other. Sweeping up his jacket, he waded toward the center of the meadow, unmindful of the frigid water saturating his socks once again.

The helicopter came up the canyon slowly, blades flashing silver from the invisible sun. Watching it glide toward them was, to Charlie, like having all her Christmases rolled up into one—the most thrilling, beautiful gift she'd ever received. Beside her, Cid was venting his excitement by hurling pebbles at the sky that swished the air going straight up and then thumped the water like sporadic hail.

Ross showed his jacket lining in bullfighter stance. Close enough to churn the water and whip Ross's hair, the helicopter's side came about; a head wearing a baseball cap, mirror sunglasses and earphones, examined the scene from the open door.

"Good morning, folks," a loudspeaker bleated. "Need a lift?"

Ross signaled thumbs-up, pointed back at Charlie and Cid.

"Three of you? No problem. How deep's the water?"

He spread his two hands about fifteen inches.

"What's under there? Is it level?"

Ross stamped in a generous ellipse, demonstrating it was.

"Holes? Rocks?"

A shrug and upturned palms.

"I can get down okay, but lifting out again is the bottom line. Maybe we better hover and bring you up on a rope."

The head disappeared and there was faint mumbling on the microphone. Charlie guessed there were two people in the cockpit conferring on how to proceed. Ross waved broadly to reclaim their attention.

"Yo. What you got?" the voice acknowledged.

Walking toward the southwest corner of the clearing, he beckoned like a traffic cop—come on, this way. He pantomimed "up" and "over," ending with a forefinger aimed at the mesa.

The helicopter tipped and followed and flitted higher. "Gottcha. You sure you can get up there?"

Ross nodded hard and signaled "safe" with his arms.

"Be right back."

They zoomed away for a landing pad inspection, and Ross sloshed back toward Charlie and Cid. "Once more into the breach, dear friends. One more river to cross."

"Just don't get in my way," Charlie warned, grinning.

She had forgotten about getting dressed, and now she danced around on one leg, trying to fit the other through uncooperative jeans. Ross went to her aid, determinedly supporting her middle. He glanced guiltily toward Cid, but Cid was already far out in the meadow, his loose-jointed gait retracing their storm route.

"What's going to happen to him?" Charlie nodded at Cid's retreating figure. "Will you press charges?"

"Will you?" Ross wished he had more hands to touch her more places at once. He let go of the gentle curve of her waist to fit his palms against the sleek lines of her jawbone.

"He needs a psychiatrist. Prison would just make him worse."

"I agree." He stroked her cool cheek with his thumbs.

"You agree with me?" she said, raising her eyebrows in a gesture of exaggerated surprise. "That's a switch."

The helicopter was coming back. Cid halted and shaded his eyes at its approach. Ross linked arms with Charlie and they went to the brink of the flood.

"Looks perfect. We'll be waiting for you," the pilot called. The helicopter bobbed and sailed away in a characteristically graceful move.

"Last one up's a rotten last one up," Charlie challenged and they began to slog after Cid with joyous, kicking steps that poured water into their boots and spattered mud up to their hair.

A jumpsuited figure appeared at the edge of the mesa, waved, and hunched his shoulders to slide his hands into his pockets. "Jesus!" came down distinctly as he pointed in the direction of Sayers Lake before Charlie and Ross waded into the original creekbed, out of sight of the overlook.

Holding hands tightly, they stumbled through the deeper, icy water. They passed a tree that had inexplicably survived the flood. Charlie braced her hand against it and gasped as it rocked, loose in its muddy socket.

On the steep rock trail, Cid's wet footprints gleamed. At the top, he and two rescuers waited, smoking cigarettes, exchanging comments full of expletives concerning the flood.

"You got room for all of us in one trip?" Ross shouted over the noise of the idling engine.

"All but George over there." The pilot tipped his head toward the Washington sculpture. "What's the story on that?"

"A hobby of my grandfather's. Could we fly by for a closer look?"

"No problem."

They loaded into the back, Charlie in the middle. The helicopter sprang off the mesa and swiveled toward Sayers Lake. In a moment, the nose was hovering ten yards from Washington's; his granite eyes returned their stares.

The pilot shook his head. "Ain't that something."

Orbiting the head, they found that the back was mostly untouched rock. Only the nape had been blasted and chiseled into a sketchy, bowed wig.

They swung around and over the lip of the cliff, past the red-brown homestead sea, down to another level. Charlie remembered it had been populated with pine trees; now it was a watery wasteland. The canyon they followed was scoured out, empty, except where debris had been trapped in bends. The swollen creek, a sluggish conveyor belt, continued to deliver branches and other flotsam to the distant valley.

Ross nudged Charlie and helped her hitch higher to see straight below to where their coffeepot, imprisoned in an eddy, did a slow pirouette.

He leaned forward to shout at the pilot, "Any casualties between here and Boulder?"

The other man angled his head, keeping his eyes on his flying. "One or two injured people."

"There was advance warning?"

"Yeah. Some guy apparently beat it down the mountain spreading the word."

Ross nodded, pleased, and sank back. He picked up Charlie's hand and transferred it to his own knee before resuming his watch out the window. "Hey, look. Whale Rock's still there."

They reached what had been the trailhead. Cid swore at the sight of his and Evan's cars, tires in the air like overturned turtles, buried up to the wheel wells in rocks and mud.

Bearing left, they followed the boulder field that had been a county highway and came upon a canted house dividing the dirty current in two. The top of an evergreen had pierced the upstream wall as cleanly as an arrow in an apple. Nearby, the family pickup hung by its rear axle from sagging telephone wires.

"Keep an eye out for anybody stranded," the pilot shouted. "We picked a woman and her son off that roof last night."

Islands of former roadway dotted the devastation. As they progressed farther toward Boulder, propane tanks and parts of buildings and cars floated on the water. Charlie blinked sadly at the body of a German shepherd outstretched on a slope, his collar chained to a fence post.

They reached the mouth of the canyon on the outskirts of Boulder, where a fan of rocks and refuse had mowed down a block of houses before spreading wider. Cluttered water lapped the foundations of the ones remaining.

The helicopter veered right, parallel with the foothills. "We're headed for the heliport at Community Hospital. Doctors'll look you over. Probably what you need worst is coffee and sandwiches."

"Amen!" Ross said for all of them.

CHARLIE SAT in a turquoise plastic chair in the emergency waiting room, sipping black coffee and watching for Ross. She ruefully surveyed her borrowed outfit— baggy white drawstring pants, cloth booties and green lab coat. Her own clothes—boots and all—had gone into the hospital's disposal system. A jovial doctor had shone light in her eyes, asked how she liked Colorado, and eased tetanus vaccine into her hip. She'd eaten two roast beef sandwiches, the first gobbled down as a necessity, the second savored slowly. She needed a bath and a few hours of sleep.

Except for a sturdy Chicano toddler and his sad-eyed mother, apparently waiting for "Pampa" to get a new cast, Charlie was alone in the echoing room. Ross, having had his own physical examination and food, was off somewhere talking to authorities about Cid's clear and present danger to society.

Her heart jigged at approaching footfalls, recognizing his step, and her tiredness dissolved in Ross's smile as he approached.

"You laughing at my getup?" she said, standing. "It looks a lot like yours."

They automatically wrapped their arms around each other. It felt natural, as though they'd been doing it all their lives.

"Come on," he said, urging her toward the door. "I've got a cab."

They walked through the main lobby, acutely aware of the interested stares of patrons and employees. The booties were not meant for outer wear; Charlie felt each grain of dirt from front door to curb. Ross reached to unlatch the door of a dusty white taxi, and she scooted across the seat to make room for him.

"Sorry. I can't come with you," he bent to tell her through the closing door. "The hospital won't hold Cid for observation unless we make a formal police complaint. I didn't mention you were a psychologist or we'd both be stuck here filling out forms. I'll be home as soon as I can." Slamming the door, he gave the address and some bedraggled bills to the cabby.

"Hey, wait." Ross tapped the window, and she rolled it down to receive a key. "Front door."

She twisted to watch as he went back inside, his imposing figure diminished by what looked like, from a distance, a clown suit.

IT WAS WONDERFUL, spending unlimited time in the luxury of electric lighting, indoor plumbing and hot running water. When she did emerge from the bathroom, she dressed in all but shoes and lay down for an equally luxurious nap.

The alarm clock that woke her was the drone of a doorbell under persistent pressure. Charlie forced her stiff legs over the side and stood up groaning, sore all over as if from flu or a fall. Shuffling through the twilight-filled house, she fumbled open the front door.

"Ross here?" Evan asked, shoving past her.

"No. I'm not sure when he'll be back." She held the door open as a hopeful hint.

"I bet he's furious with me, huh?"

Charlie found the light switch and brought the neat, cozy living room out of hiding. "We haven't really discussed you."

Ignoring the unenthusiastic reception, Evan crossed the carpet and dropped himself onto the sofa. "It was dumb. My not telling Ross about Cid. Him and his CIA fantasies and his manic-depressive moods. He scared me, if you want to know the truth."

"What could you have told Ross?"

"About a week ago Cid announced he was doing this special project for extra credit in government, and Dr. Wilt, his advisor, knew all about it. He was bugging our phone. For practice. He said it wasn't illegal, long as I knew about it."

"So Cid heard about me coming to Colorado. And the birthday party."

"Yeah. Then Monday, Cid and I had this big argument after we saw you in Ross's office, about whether he should practice his tailing skills on you. And when we got home, it comes out that he'd lifted Ross's grandmother's journal while I wasn't watching. That's when I told him to move out and he did, Monday night."

"And Tuesday—"

"When I was standing at the door after seeing you guys out, I spotted Cid parked up the street. Sure enough, when you drove off, he did, too. So it dawned on me what was going on. He'd found out about the treasure and planned to cut himself in. The more I thought about the two of you up there except for maybe slippery Cid, the creepier I felt. So Wednesday morning I decided to see if you were okay."

"And a good thing, too." She smiled, but he didn't notice.

"Can you believe it? I called Dr. Wilt while I was still trying to decide whether to come up there after you, and he said Cid dropped out of school four weeks ago! Wilt didn't know a thing about any bugging project. Boy, did Cid have my number—number one stupid nerd."

"Evan, it took plenty of intelligence and courage to run ahead of the flood and warn people. You're a hero."

He smiled the first real smile she'd ever seen on his face. "Not one person was killed. There aren't many houses till you get to the city limits, but still there could have been fifty or sixty killed. I was yelling through the bullhorn and tooting the van horn and thinking about the victims of the Big Thompson flood who didn't believe the warnings to get to higher ground. I guess there were others thinking of Thompson too, because they all made the effort to escape. The sheriff says I'll get a commendation."

"You see?"

Evan pushed himself to his feet. "God! I came here set to apologize and throw myself on Ross's mercy, but I don't think I can face him yet. Would you talk to him for me?"

Involuntarily, Charlie made a face.

"Please?"

"Okay. But I don't really have any influence over him."

"Just give him one of your gorgeous smiles." Evan stuck his right hand out, and Charlie, startled, shook it. "Tell him I'll bring his van back tomorrow." In the next moment, he was out of the door and bounding toward the street, calling over his shoulder, "Watch me on tonight's news, any channel!"

CHARLIE SMOOTHED her hair and checked her shirttail, seeing from the kitchen window the taxi turn into the driveway. Ross's blond head ducked clear of the passenger side, he paid the driver, and then he was striding to the front door. She sat still, savoring the sound of his footsteps coming toward the kitchen.

"You didn't lock the front door," he scolded, going to the cupboard to take down a cup.

"Sorry. Evan was just here, and I forgot, when he left."

"What did he have to say for himself?"

"He's very contrite. Says he should have warned you about Cid. He'll return the van tomorrow. What about Cid?"

"The hospital has a ward for mentally disturbed patients. They're searching for a relative who could commit him to a more long-term facility. Otherwise, you and I will have to testify to what he tried to do, to keep him off the streets." He slumped at the table, resting his chin on his hand.

"You're out on your feet. Why don't you take a shower and get some sleep?" Charlie smiled at the boyish tuft of hair bristling at attention on top of his head.

"I'll have the shower. Then we'll see." He flipped his eyebrows in a Groucho Marx leer, but the cautious way he got to his feet told Charlie he wasn't as dangerous as he pretended.

9

AFTER TWENTY MINUTES of dreamily contemplating the bubbles in her second cup of coffee, Charlie tiptoed down the hall and peeped in at Ross's unclosed room. He lay on his face on the bed, still wearing borrowed clothes— shower apparently delayed.

Feeling the ambiguous sensations of tenderness and disappointment, she went to her own room. Undressing, enjoying the smooth coolness of the sheets on her skin, she settled down to get more sleep. The last thing she did was to pry open an eye to check that she'd left the hall door ajar.

And in her dreams, he came to her.

He touched her hair, her earlobe, the side of her throat, one shoulder. As the dream began to slip away, she moaned a protest, wanting it to go on. Wanting him to go on.

The wraithlike hand drifted under the sheet, following the line of her shoulder blade into the small of her back. His fingers spread wide across the flair of her hip. Lower. The sheet lifted off her body, and she sighed, more awake than asleep now, feeling his eyes and his breath as well as his hands on her. She arched her back with pleasure as his fingers trailed around her rib cage and brushed the underside of her breast.

"Guess who." His words feathered against her cheek and made her mouth curve.

"It's Prince Charming," she murmured, enjoying the little shocks of excitation his wandering hand had set off.

He buried his face in her neck and nibbled the skin. She laughed and rolled toward him, wrapping her arms around his back, looking into his blue eyes inches from her own.

"I'm ticklish there," she complained.

He was bare to the waist. His crisp, golden chest brushed her naked breasts as he lowered himself to kiss her mouth. She stroked his muscled back and upper arms, floating in the euphoria of pure feeling.

"You're not going to stop me this time, are you?" he rasped.

"Not on your life," Charlie promised.

"This is your last chance."

"Oh, I hope not," she breathed, and, dragging his head down with her fingers laced in his damp hair, she kissed him the desperate, demanding kiss of a woman racked with desire.

Boldly, she moved one hand from his hair to locate the snap of his waistband, slid the zipper down, and gently freed him through the opening she'd made. Together, they pushed the jeans down and away and clung to each other unhampered, arms, legs, mouths.

Abruptly he drew back, letting cool air come between their upper bodies. She clutched at him, eyes flying open, protest on the tip of her tongue.

"Shh. I want to look at you."

And he did, by the dim light fanning through the hall door. "Beautiful. You're beautiful." He rested the back of one hand on her collarbone and trailed it lightly down between her breasts, rolled it over to cover her left breast.

His fingers explored the areola, drawing weightless circles.

"Ahh," she breathed as his warm mouth found the other breast to lick and suck and gently bite. "Ross? Ross!"

She couldn't lie still. The delectable torment made her arch her hips. He trapped her flailing legs under one of his and continued with the relentless arousal. Rougher now, yet careful not to hurt her, he teased each breast with the briefest abrasion of the stubble on his jaw. Every jerk of her body fed his own desire. He couldn't stop now if she'd begged him.

But she was begging for something else entirely. Her sighs had turned to rising demands for release. "Please, I need you inside me," she repeated, straining toward him.

He hissed through his teeth and with Herculean effort pushed her away from him.

"What are you doing?" she cried. She suddenly imagined he was going to pay her back for the times she'd refused his lovemaking. He wasn't going to finish what he'd started!

His response seemed to confirm it. "Whoa! Is this the shy and oh-so-cool psychologist I couldn't seduce for love or money?"

She tried to focus her eyes and gave up, closing them, instead. "I don't recall you offering money," she joked automatically, willing the throb in her pelvis to stop.

The bed jiggled, and she felt him reaching across her for his jeans. She bit her lip and tried more levity. "Okay, what if I offer you money?"

"That would be great, but you better take delivery first. In case you aren't satisfied."

She heard the crackle of cellophane and raised one eyelid.

"Speaking of deliveries," he said, showing her the package, "I promised you no babies."

She smiled broadly, thankful she'd misjudged him, grateful he'd remembered the protection.

"Let me do it," she said, hoping he didn't recognize the contriteness in her voice.

She sheathed him slowly, her fingertips lightly exploring and massaging until his hand clamped her wrist, making her wait while he regained control.

After a minute, he raised himself up on an elbow and forced her backward and under him. "Now, where were we?"

She brought one of his hands to her breast. "Here?"

"Good choice. And I think thumb and finger were like so—"

She reacted with a gasp and a shudder as violent as it was involuntary.

Ross grinned down at her. "Yes, that must have been it." He shifted to look the length of her body. "But let's see what else is here, shall we?"

He laid his other hand on the soft triangle between her legs and began a lazy caress, long fingers sliding farther and deeper with each pass. He could feel her pulsating under the strokes, each drag of his hand making her tremble harder. She was pleading with him to enter her, but he knew he'd explode on the first thrust.

Instead, he stopped her demands with a kiss, and his hand continued its delicate furrowing. And when he felt her stiffen and bare her teeth, he lifted his hips and drove himself into her. Once. Again. Three times.

Her tensed body buckled, her mouth ripped away from his, and he felt her convulsions as if they were his own. Then they *were* his own, he was panting and groaning with her, and the waves of release echoed again and again and again.

THEY LAY INTERTWINED and spent, their breathing slowing. Beside her ear, Charlie experienced the steady thump of his heart, feeling her own heart decelerate.

"You okay?" he asked, tracing her cheekbone with a fingertip.

"I'm great," she sighed.

"True, but not very modest of you to say so." Ross slid his hand across her ear and deep into her disheveled hair. "And *I* was pretty good too, wasn't I?" He had a fleeting urge to beat on his chest.

"Who's immodest now?" Charlie pushed up to look him in the eye. "And what was all that tommyrot about you not being experienced at seducing women?"

"Did I say that?"

"Two nights ago when you were trying to make me feel sorry for you so I'd let you in my bed."

"Oh. Then." He wound his elbow around her neck to haul her down to his shoulder again. "Promise you won't get mad?"

"Oh-oh, this is going to be good," Charlie said, idly twirling his chest hair, liking the wiry-silky contrast of it.

"The reason I didn't know how to seduce you was because in the past, the woman seduced me. Hey, you promised not to laugh."

"I didn't laugh. It was more of a snort."

They shared ten minutes of companionable silence before, unwillingly, Charlie began to think about the time. This was Thursday night or Friday morning—she was too comfortable to check the clock—and she had to fly home on Sunday. Too soon! Depression coursed through her. She'd never see Ross again. The thought rocked her head on his shoulder, a helpless negation of what she knew would be the future.

"What's the matter?"

"My arm's gone to sleep," she invented.

She hitched herself to a kneeling position next to his hip and began to massage his flat stomach, deliberately shaking off anguish, determined to make the most of the hours left. When she bent to kiss the dark nipples of his tanned chest, the surrounding golden hair tickled her cheek. She slid lower and put her tongue in his navel.

Charlie lifted her head and saw he'd shut his eyes to concentrate on the pleasurable sensation. "You aren't going to stop me, are you?" she murmured, mouthing warm, wet kisses down his stomach.

His mouth twitched toward a smile.

"This is your last chance," she warned, continuing her progress downward.

The smile grew and one glittering eye peered at her.

She turned her face into the valley between his torso and thigh, letting her hand drift to where the hair thickened, running her fingers through it before cupping the velvety center that responded at once, beginning to swell. She drew deep breaths of his wonderful, masculine scent, musky and warm.

Enjoy it now, Charlie, her treacherous mind reared up to say. *It's going to be pure torture remembering it in Chicago.* Abruptly she swayed to her knees, making the mattress shimmy. To answer his questioning look, she commanded him to roll over.

Straddling his hips, she started a leisurely exploration of his muscles, kneading him with careful fingertips and nails, his neck, shoulders, arms, back. Her hands skirted a yellow-black bruise under his left shoulder blade, a temporary brand acquired on the mountain. She dropped a feathery kiss on the mark before turning around to massage his feet, ankles, calf muscles, knees, thighs.

Ross lay suspended in time and space, engrossed by Charlie's hands heating his skin and her smooth thighs riding his waist. He was extremely content. But he also felt stirrings in his groin, intimations of renewing need.

It had been a long time since he couldn't get his fill of a woman. Come to think of it, there'd never been such a time. But here he was, as randy as a teenager, eager to couple with Charlie a second time. And after that he'd hold her till he'd regenerated enough to take her again, as many times as the night's hours would allow, never tiring of her, never reaching satiation.

And tomorrow night and the next and—

Ross's thoughts pulled up short at the mental image of a plane carrying Charlie east. In a few months, another flight would take him west, doubling the distance between them.

Could she care enough about him to give up her own work and join him in California? Would he miss her enough to ask her to do that? What if he missed her that much and she refused?

"Loosen up," Charlie chided softly. "I won't hurt you."

Ross relaxed, letting her soothe his brain as well as his body. Like Scarlett O'Hara, he'd think about it tomorrow.

"Now flip over and I'll do your front," she said, transferring her weight to her knees to let him turn between her thighs.

He studied her slender back while she rubbed tension out of his legs. He spread his palms on her waist, fitting his fingers into the depressions between her ribs.

She glanced back at him and smiled shyly. "Your legs seem less tense, but your—other areas—are—"

"I noticed." He dragged a forefinger down her spine and was rewarded with her squirm of response. "Ready for another round?"

She tipped sideways off him and stroked his chest, the other hand supporting her head. "Don't you want the rest of your rubdown first?"

"If you'd lie on top of me and wiggle around, you could cover more territory at once."

"You want quantity instead of quality?" She shook her head in disbelief.

He smiled at the one breast he could see pointing pertly at his heart. His grasp followed his gaze. "Quality? This is first-class material right here."

Twitching reflexively, she shut her eyes on the primitive signal her nipple sent to her pelvis. "Don't distract me from my work," she forced past gritted teeth as, seeing her reaction, he repeated that particular series of moves. She groped down his body to the hard proof of their mutual craving. "This is also first-class," she tried to say, her tongue thick and clumsy.

The slow movements of Charlie's hand brought Ross's desire to the brink, and his fingers roughened on her breast, giving her pleasure that bordered on pain. When he released her long enough to deal with contraception, she pressed her own hand where his had been, as if to preserve the sensations he'd provoked.

When he whispered, "Let me in," she spread her legs so readily, so gladly, that he paused, struck with wonder at his good fortune. She watched him, puzzled, and he settled over her.

"Just admiring the view," he told her, fitting his body into hers and sliding deep, then deeper.

What had been a wild disco dance the first time was this time rich and stately. They kissed and touched with the unhurried languor of an underwater ballet. Their sweat-slickened bodies buffed together and apart so smoothly, the bed scarcely moved. Silent too, except for sighs, they approached and retreated from climax repeatedly, prolonging anticipation of the moment when they couldn't possibly resist one moment longer.

Ross felt the first thrill begin, like a roller coaster hanging for a second at the top of the swoop. "Charlie!" he cried.

She dug her nails into his skin and let his writhing drop her over the edge, too, matching him shudder for shudder.

When they could think again, they shared an amazed stare.

Ross swallowed on a very dry throat. "Two for two."

"A good score," Charlie punned. "We make a good team."

"Yeah." He hugged her to him and gazed past her shoulder at nothing, unsure whether he wanted to laugh or cry.

They slept. When the sun painted the window blind orange, they woke and made love and ate breakfast and made love again. They lay on their sides like spoons in a silverware box, her back nestled tightly against his front.

"Are you sore from all this handling?" His words brushed her ear. "Does it feel raw here? Or here? Or down here?"

"I can take it if you can take it," Charlie said, reaching behind herself to touch some of Ross's more vulnerable spots. "Are you numb there, maybe?"

"Just give me a minute to catch my breath," he bragged. "I have not yet begun to fight."

"How about regretting you have but one life to give?"

"You've got it wrong. This sex stuff adds years to a person's life. The exercise. The burning of calories. The exhausted sleep in between."

She scrubbed her bottom against him and smiled. After a few minutes of pensive silence, she asked, "What are you going to do about the Washington carving?"

"I'm not sure. Get somebody from the art department to come look at it. And somebody from engineering. To see if it's feasible to move it."

"To a museum?"

"I don't know. I may not have any say in what happens to it. I need to find out whether Boulder or the Forest Service wants to claim it."

The sound of the kitchen telephone floated up the hall. They both moaned. Ross shoved out of bed and began to drag on his jeans.

"How come we've been so lucky the phone didn't ring before now?" Charlie wondered.

"Probably because I disconnected the bell till breakfast this morning." Ross slapped his palm on the door frame as he went through, ordering over his shoulder, "Save my place."

The bed was chilly and hard without Ross. When he didn't return right away, she got up, threw on her robe, and walked toward the murmur of his voice. As words became distinguishable, she could tell he wasn't talking to Brenda or anyone else requiring privacy, so she slipped into the kitchen to draw a glass of cold water.

"We were up there camping." Ross covered the mouthpiece and stage-whispered, "Reporter."

Charlie nodded and yawned shamelessly.

"I'm not sure she wants her name in the paper. Let me ask." Ross muffled the receiver again and raised his eyebrows.

"It isn't a supermarket scandal rag, is it?" she asked suspiciously.

"Local daily."

She shrugged. "I don't care if you don't care."

"Charlie Yost," Ross said into the phone. "*C-h-a-r-l-i-e.* A friend visiting from Chicago." He listened momentarily. "Right. He was a stranger we met on the trail up there shortly before all hell broke loose."

Charlie chuckled, appreciating the inside joke.

"No, I'm not sure how you can get in touch with him."

Ross pantomimed wanting a drink of her water, and Charlie knocked back the last in the glass before rinsing and refilling it. She couldn't resist, after she handed it over, letting her knuckles brush down his chest, admiring his throat as he tilted his head to drink. Her forefinger dipped inside the waist of his jeans to wipe back and forth along his warm belly.

"No, I really don't think pictures are necessary. I'd rather not." He frowned at the floor, listening. "Maybe. Hold on." He held the receiver to his chest. "You willing to say a few words to the fourth estate? He wants to know how it felt to be wet and cold and scared."

Charlie laughed.

"Don't mention George Washington," Ross said, handing her the receiver.

"Hello, this is Charlie Yost," she said, nodding.

"Good morning," a young, energetic, male voice leaped into her ear. "I understand you're one of the three flood survivors who was up near Chokecherry Lake when it breached."

"That's right."

"Would you describe how you became aware of the danger? What did you hear and see?"

"Ross and I were beside a creek that runs below the two lakes, and suddenly I knew the dam was about to break and we should go get Cid and move to higher ground."

"Wait a minute. You're saying you *knew* it was going to break before it actually did?"

"Uh, it seemed that way. It all happened very fast," she rationalized, glancing uneasily at Ross.

"You're visiting Colorado for the first time?" the reporter asked, failing to follow up. He sounded very young.

"Yes, first time," Charlie agreed.

"What do you do back in Chicago?"

"I'm working on a master's degree at the University of Chicago."

"Uh-huh. In what field?"

"Paranormal psychology."

There was silence on the line, and she glanced up to find Ross waving his hand and shaking his head in the universal "stop" signal.

The reporter said, "You mean ESP and mind reading and that kind of stuff?"

"Yes," she said, narrowing her eyes at Ross's agitation.

"Oh. Well. Are you, yourself, clairvoyant? Did you know the dam was about to burst before it really happened?"

"By a few minutes, yes."

Ross grasped the phone cord and tugged it gently, his other hand motioning she should hand it over. She turned her back, frowning.

"So what told you? I mean—" the writer groped for what to ask.

"I happened to touch the creek water, which gave me a psychic vision of the trickling dam."

Ross thumped his empty glass onto the counter so hard, Charlie's spine snapped to attention.

"Hey, this is great! I really need a picture and an in-depth interview, Ms. Yost. Could I meet with you today?"

"No, I really don't think—"

"I promise not to take much of your time. Ten minutes."

"I'm sorry, no. My schedule is extremely tight. Thanks anyway for your interest. Here's Dr. Davies."

She thrust the receiver at him, but Ross was slow to take it, preoccupied with glaring at her. Growling, "Sorry, I've got to hang up now. Goodbye. No. No. Goodbye," he replaced the phone with unnecessary force. "I could have told you he'd be a pest if you let him get wind of this psychic thing."

Charlie folded her arms and lifted her chin. "You weren't afraid of him being a pest. You were afraid of the public reading about my line of work."

"I didn't want you to be embarrassed—"

"You mean *you* didn't want to be embarrassed! You're ashamed of what I do. You don't understand it, and you're scared to even admit the field merits study. I can just imagine you introducing me at a faculty party, avoiding any reference to my career. You'd have everyone thinking I was a hooker. You'd rather that I was a hooker!"

She twisted away and got as far as two steps down the hall before his hand grabbed her wrist and spun her around, backing her into the wall. A hand on either side of her head, not touching her, he stared into eyes that sparkled on the verge of tears. Immediately, all his anger was for himself.

"Charlie, don't be mad at me. I'll try harder. I promise."

"It doesn't matter whether you believe in me or not." Charlie shook her head dully. "You and I are going our different ways. I didn't expect to make you a believer, but I am disappointed that I couldn't even make you an agnostic."

"You've only had a few days to work on me."

"And they've been exciting in more ways than one. But in spite of everything we've done together—" she swallowed "—we're going to say goodbye soon and return to our regular lives, and this week together will gradually fade from our minds. So whether you think I'm psychic or not, it doesn't matter."

She braced herself and let her eyes drift up to his face, past the set mouth, the lean cheek, to his blue, blue eyes. "You will send me a Christmas card, won't you?" She tried to smile.

"There must be a way we can change that scenario," Ross protested softly. "Maybe you could come out to California to—to visit. Perhaps look for a job out there."

"Why?" she asked with deliberate cruelty. "I've got a job. And friends who accept me for what I am. Why should I chase after someone who doesn't?"

"God, Charlie. What am I going to do without you?" He looked at her mouth as if he could taste it.

Her stomach fluttered, and she wanted to fall against him and beg him to love her. Instead, she stood very still and said, "It's not me you want. You see good legs and a nice figure and they turn you on. But there's more to me than sex, Ross. I'm a package deal, a body plus a mind. You don't like the way I think. Someday the body won't be as beautiful, and what would be left for you to admire?"

She pushed lightly against his right arm and he gave way, letting her walk down the hall. She couldn't resist one backward look. He still leaned on one arm, head bowed in an attitude of dejection that made her ache to hold and comfort him. But the best gift she could give him, she knew, was a clean break. So she went into her bedroom and quietly closed the door.

As the latch snapped, the telephone rang. Charlie grabbed up her clothes and began to dress. She hurried, afraid Ross might come in before she finished, afraid he might destroy her resolution.

But she was fully covered, brushing her hair, when his tap sounded on the door. "I have to go out," he called.

"Okay," she answered, frozen in front of the mirror, brush poised at the crown of her head.

"I won't be long. Brenda—"

Charlie lowered the brush, staring into her own wide, unhappy eyes. "Okay," she repeated.

"Brenda's car won't start, so I'm going to take her to the grocery store. She'll pay us back with a spaghetti supper tonight."

"All right," she said, for variety.

His steps withdrew, returned. "You need anything?"

"No. Thank you."

She heard him moving around the house, jingling keys, opening the garage door. What had to be the motor of his aunt's car ground into action, and the sound dwindled into silence.

Not letting herself reconsider, Charlie snatched up her belongings and stuffed them into suitcases. The cosmetics case full of books was too much to handle. She put it in the middle of the crumpled bed with a scribbled note of explanation. Giving the room a last sweep with her eyes, not allowing them to linger on the forlorn little case surrounded by love-tangled sheets, she left, carefully locking the front door behind her.

As she tried to hurry down the street, the suitcases slapped awkwardly at her legs, the purse strap kept sliding off her shoulder, and her nose needed blowing. She bit her lip and kept walking downhill toward town, watching for a public phone, anxious to get inside somewhere in case Ross used this route coming home. She didn't want the hurt and embarrassment of another confrontation. This was like trying to escape the flood—except the flood had threatened her life and Ross only threatened her sanity.

After six long blocks of residential district, she came to a busy through street and set the bags down to flex her shoulders. A car zoomed to the curb almost in front of her, a taxi dropping off passengers. Leaving the luggage where it lay, Charlie ran waving to the driver. He waited, head ducked low to see her approaching the curbside window.

"I need a ride," she panted. "Is there a shuttle to the Denver airport from Boulder?"

"Yes, ma'am, there's one every half hour from the Holiday Inn."

"Wait," she demanded and dashed to get her cases and heave them into the back door he opened from inside.

Flicking on the meter, he pulled into traffic, right arm draped nonchalantly over the seat. "I could take you to Stapleton. Wouldn't cost much more than the limousine. Quicker."

She hesitated, thinking of how much less trouble it would be to go directly to Denver. She said, "No, thank you. I'll take the shuttle."

"You be the boss," he observed, his tone indicating she wasn't a particularly clever one.

She sank into the cheap upholstery, missing Ross already. She could probably beat him home, and he would never know she'd tried to, literally, run away from the problem of loving him. But she couldn't go back, couldn't bear being with him any longer, knowing that their relationship was a hopeless dead end. The healing couldn't start until the wounding stopped; she imagined the healing would take a long, long time.

TEN BLOCKS SOUTHWEST, Ross was helping Brenda carry groceries to her door.

"I'm going to miss you," she said, before tucking her wallet into her mouth to free her key hand.

"With your looks and cooking skills, you'll have a chump to take my place in no time." He bounced the sacks higher on his chest and shouldered through the door behind her.

"See? He even talks to me like a brother." Their rubber soles squeaked on the wooden floor. "It's been nice of Mandy to share you."

Ross bumped the sacks onto the kitchen table. "Want me to have a look at the car?"

"Naw. Maybe tonight after supper you could see if it's anything obvious. You come at six and not a minute sooner. I'm breaking in a new gentleman friend tonight, so please be on your best behavior."

"Anyone I know?"

They strolled toward the front door, his arm draped across her shoulders.

"Jim Granby, English lit associate prof. Know him?"

Ross stepped out on the porch. "No, but he sounds like a winner. Anything you want me to bring?"

"An appetite. Charlie."

Ross paused in his tracks, thought a moment, and turned around. "How'd you like to give me a little sisterly advice?"

"Are you kidding? Don't I always?"

"Do you think I should agree with Charlie that she's psychic when I don't believe such an ability even exists? Lie to make her happy?"

Brenda cocked her head, considering. "Why do you want to make her happy? So she'll do you favors?"

Ross drew himself up and huffed, "Certainly not." He slumped. "Well, maybe. She seems to have gotten under my skin."

"Yeah?" Brenda grinned suggestively. "Anywhere else?"

"Come on, Bren, I'm in pain here."

She studied his face. "So I see. No, Ross, I don't think you should lie. I think you should study up on paranormal phenomena. Give it a chance. Maybe you'll find aspects of it you can concede possible. Heck, maybe you'll accept it lock, stock, line and sinker. Go into the crystal ball business."

"Yeah. Study it." Ross made a face like a small boy confronting liver for dinner. "Well, see you." And he jumped the steps two at a time to the street.

CHARLIE WAS HANDING her two suitcases to a smartly uniformed driver and climbing into a sleek black limousine.

She'd been lucky enough to catch the ride and the last available seat, as the driver was glancing at his watch, one hand on the door handle. The other passengers, suited and briefcased, nodded curtly before resuming their discussion of prototypes and data bases. Grateful for anonymity, and for making progress in her escape, she stared out her window at the mountains, wondering if she'd have any trouble changing to an earlier flight.

AS ROSS REENTERED the house, he sensed its too-quiet atmosphere and called out for Charlie. He came to the open bedroom door and saw the gray cosmetics case squatting ominously on the bed, the white scrap of paper on top beckoning him to come confirm what he'd already guessed: "Sorry to be such a coward, but I hate good-byes. Please send this case of propaganda to me C.O.D. No hurry. Thanks for everything." He tore it into confetti before striding to telephone Brenda.

CHARLIE'S LUCK continued to hold at the ticket counter, where a young woman with a complexion as smooth and brown as cocoa did mysterious things to Charlie's ticket, transforming it from a Sunday to a Friday flight. With over an hour to kill, Charlie went directly to the departure gate, where she took a seat in a corner by the windows and dug a paperback out of her shoulder bag and pretended to read.

"SHOULD I CALL THE AIRPORT?" Ross asked Brenda over the telephone. "Maybe I did or said something that hurt her feelings. I must have. I did. I hate to let her go like this. Hell, I hate to let her go, period."

"From what you've told me," Brenda's voice stroked his ear, "I'd say she just didn't see any future in prolonging her time in Colorado. I can sympathize with that."

"But she didn't have to go till Sunday. We could have had a couple more days together." And nights, he added to himself.

"She either doesn't care for you or she cares more than she wants to. Got any clues which it might be?"

For a panicky moment, Ross couldn't speak; a toss of a coin would have been as accurate as his answer. "I'll have to mull it over," he said, noticing the water glass on the counter, thinking that it bore the imprints of her hands and mouth. "Bye, Brenda. Don't let Jim Granby do anything I wouldn't do."

"You better make me a list."

Putting up the receiver, he held the glass to the light before depositing it among the other dirty dishes in the washer.

CHARLIE BOARDED the plane, out of range of the terminal's loudspeaker system with its endless litany of names of persons wanted on a white courtesy phone. She was both relieved and disappointed that her name had not been announced.

AT THAT MOMENT, Ross sat in his office, which looked as if the flood had come through it, talking on the phone again. "Hey, Kevin. Ross... Not much, how about you? I was hoping you could take a high country hike with me. I've got something I'd like you to see. Give me your expert opinion on." Ross listened, managed to chuckle. "Oh, you heard about my last hike. It wasn't the most fun date I've ever had, that's for sure." He rubbed at pain above his eyes. "No, you heard right. The woman thinks she's—" He tensed a muscle in his jaw and forced himself to test the sound of it. "The lady is a paranormal psychologist. And she's honest-to-gosh psychic."

10

JUNE IN CHICAGO RAINED. The days, like Charlie's life, plodded by, gray and relentlessly dull. After the initial excitement of describing the flood and the discovery of the carving to Mandy, Charlie didn't want to talk about Colorado anymore. She didn't want to think about it. She wanted time to pass and distance her emotions from the days she'd spent with Ross.

Leafing through a magazine and coming across a photograph of mountains, any mountains, jabbed her under the ribs. When lightning accompanied the rain and rolled thunder through Chicago's streets, Charlie caught her breath, momentarily shivering on a high trail. A stranger's low laugh, or a glimpse of unruly blond hair could sting her eyes and close her throat.

She was stoic, determined to get on with her life. At first Mandy had plied her with questions, impossible questions such as what did she think of Ross. But the answers were too pat and brief, so that Mandy, reading between the lines, stopped pestering for details of the visit.

July. The city baked by day and simmered by night. Charlie threw herself into her studies. Every project or scientific test her colleagues mentioned, she pursued with unflagging dedication. At night, she sat propped up in bed weighted down with literature on the paranormal, reading till the threat of insomnia had passed.

On a Friday afternoon in the last week of July, Mandy breezed into the apartment and flapped mail at Charlie, who was dozing on the living-room couch over a new library book about psychic animals.

"A postcard from Mother in Rome, the spoiled broad. A Christmas catalog, can you believe it? And a padded mailer to both of us from Ross."

The name hadn't lost its ability to make Charlie's chest constrict. "Oh?" She flexed the spine of her book and stared fixedly at the same unreadable line.

"Shall I open it?" Mandy asked airily.

"It'll make it a lot easier to figure out what he sent."

The package rustled an interminable time. Mandy sank into the opposite end of the couch and read from a typewritten page, "'Dear Mandy and Charlie, especially Mandy since she hasn't seen it—here is a photo of the Sayers tiara and the Davies gem.'"

Mandy dug into the envelope and produced the picture. "Washington and Ross," she crowed. "What a class act." She handed the photograph to Charlie and read on. "'Work is underway to move the head. Boulder wants to repair both dams and refill the lakes, but there's enough interest in the Washington to finance a relocation down to the homestead meadow. Maybe all the way to a city park eventually.'"

Charlie had finally steeled herself to look at the photo. Ross stood beside the carving, his head below the cantilever of Washington's nose. Ross was grinning, head ducked low and hands in pockets, like a self-conscious boy. Her fingers tingled, feeling the texture of his wind-mussed hair.

"'Haven't found any other carvings—sorry, Charlie—but, as you can see, this one would have taken

Grandfather quite a while.'" Mandy glanced at Charlie's expressionless face and continued, "'The weather has been monotonously gorgeous.'"

Charlie thought about the animals. She was dead certain they represented Noah's ark and signified the flood. Not this summer's disaster, but the first flood, when the carving of Washington and his immediate surroundings had disappeared under the lake. But Ross would never concede that. He'd sneer at a comparison between ESP and the symbolism of dreams.

Mandy, fishing in the mailer again, brought out a manila coin envelope and passed it to Charlie. Ross had written a note on one side, the words squeezed small to fit:

> Charlie—here's a souvenir from the base of the statue. The soil is full of these stone chips.
>
> Merry Christmas
>
> R.

She tore the end across and tipped the contents into her lap. The oblong wafer of gray-white stone was almost weightless. Turning it over, she found the chisel marks, like a giant's fingerprint embedded in the granite.

"'. . . digging it out,'" Mandy was reading, "'or tunneling under. We'll probably use a stone saw at the base.'"

The granite tickled her palm like a Mexican jumping bean. Oh, no, you don't, Charlie thought. No more memories. No more looking into Ross Davies's antecedents. She tossed the chip onto the glass coffee table at her knees.

Mandy tucked the letter into its envelope. "That's nice. He doesn't write very often." She leaned to inspect the sliver of rock. "Too light for a paperweight. How about drilling a hole in it and making it into a pendant?"

"I expect it'll end up as yet another curio to be dusted," Charlie said tactlessly, insulating herself with disinterest.

Mandy sent her a look that Charlie recognized, with horror, as pity. Ostentatiously, she reopened her book and propped her head on her fist in an attitude of concentration.

"Charlie, you remember I'm going to spend the weekend with David and some other people at his cabin on the lake?"

"Right, I remember." Charlie put her feet on the couch, noticed the photo lying beside her, and held it out.

"You keep it," Mandy said, waving it away.

Opening her mouth to refuse, she heard herself say, "Okay. Thanks," and felt her arm stretch to put it beside the piece of granite.

Determinedly, she began to read, moving her lips to assure progress: *It seems reasonable that pets, loving their masters, become attuned to their humans' moods and thoughts much as two people who love each other are more physically sensitive than are two strangers. Love sharpens psychic awareness.*

Charlie sighed and shut the book. Love sharpens everything, she thought dejectedly. Love itself has an edge that can draw invisible blood.

Later Mandy called her to supper—it was Mandy's week to cook—and later still, Mandy called goodbye as David patted out "Shave and a Haircut" on his car horn. From her bedroom, which was really Mrs. Davies's bedroom, Charlie answered with the standard good wishes for fun and safety.

Doors banged, voices welcomed, motors started. After a few minutes, the apartment was as silent as bated breath. Charlie stirred the air with a hanger, putting away the last of a load of laundry she'd done earlier. She upended the empty basket against her hip and drummed the bottom, deliberating.

Like a sleepwalker, she glided through doorways, into the living room, up to the coffee table. She fumbled Ross's picture into the pocket of her robe without looking at it. The bit of granite seemed to leap into her palm. Charlie gave the resigned sigh of an addict yielding to temptation and sat down with the granite warming in her hand.

THE SUN WAS HIGH and white, and the sky was an outrageous blue between fluffy white clouds. A dignified breeze, soft and steady, rumpled the tall grass. Red rock outcroppings, like rusty relics, lay strewn about the field. One ghostly boulder, as big as the cabin on the trail below, had summoned him here.

The old man hunkered beside it on the shaded side, wielding his knife gracefully, dicing sticks of dynamite into shorter lengths. He whistled tunelessly as the blade bounced sunlight off rocks and tree trunks and his own face.

A short-haired, plume-tailed dog came sniffing across the rubble to whine and wag a greeting.

"Yes, yes," the man said, using the knife handle to scratch behind his friend's ears. He straightened up and combed a weathered hand through his graying beard. "Lessee here," he said, laying the cut dynamite in a neat row in front of his scuffed boots. "One, two, three, four, five, by golly."

The dog looked interested and squirmed his hind-quarters.

The man wiped his hands on his black wool trousers, hiked his suspenders higher on his shoulders and selected a fuse from a handy table of rock. One tail of the fuse had been crimped to a blasting cap that he now tamped into the end of the first stick of dynamite.

George Washington gazed with oblivious patience into the distance.

The artist talked to his canine companion as he inserted one plug of explosive into a hole he'd bored in the base of the boulder. "See here where there's too much rock in the small of George's back? And lower, here? We can't have the Father of America looking too stout. Nossir."

He stepped away to inspect his work, the bore hole loaded with dynamite, the fuse dangling out, and the mouth of the hole stoppered with damp dirt brought up from the truck garden.

"Now that should about do it. Nothing too lively, just a little sneeze of nitroglycerin," he said, eyes reflecting his anticipation. "You go over there behind that rock tooth and wait for me. Go on."

The pointing finger shook impatiently, and the dog slunk away. A sulphur match was struck, the fuse was lit, and the man danced awkwardly to safety. He wrapped fingers in the dog's furry chest till the eruption peppered their hiding place with pebbles and dust.

He went to inspect the cavity, rubbing at the still warm surface with his bare hand. "You see here? That's nigh perfect. Let's do her four times more."

He set the other charges in their bore holes, fused, tamped and stoppered them, and stepped back to squint

*critically and tell the dog that no one could have done it
better than Tim. He lit the fuses one after another and
galloped to cover just ahead of the first concussion. The
dog flinched under his hand as another blast and another echoed the first and ricocheted off the canyon
walls. As the noise rolled away, a new sound blended
with it and rose in volume.*

"Timothy! Timothy!"

*He scuttled up the smooth stone slope overlooking his
cabin. Elizabeth stood directly below, her face upturned, hands cupped around her eyes.*

"Well?" he sent down.

*"The baby's took a fall out of the loft. It appears his
arm is broke."*

*"Coming!" He was already backing down the incline,
and the dog romped ahead of him down the trail.*

LIKE A PROJECTOR out of film, the vision ended. Charlie
shook off the spell, becoming aware of the coffee table
pressed against her shins and the granite chip biting into
her too-tight fist. She sank back into the couch, feeling
privileged to have shared an episode in Ross's grandparents' lives.

The longer she reflected, the less satisfied she was.
Something nagged at her; something she'd seen was
wrong. Charlie considered the flake of granite in her
hand, and when no new idea came, she set it on the
tabletop and swayed tiredly to bed.

The scene began, an instant replay at normal speed,
filling her sleeping mind. The perfect summer day in
Colorado high country. The man in his rough work
clothes, slicing dynamite as casually as if it were carrot
sticks. The dog. The explosions—whump, whump,

whump, whump. The wife's light voice carrying to the husband whose help she needed. The baby's broken arm. Fade-out.

Charlie struggled to sit up; her limbs tangled in the bedclothes had frightened her, making her think for a moment before her head cleared that she was Cid's prisoner again. She switched on the bedside lamp.

What did it mean, first the vision and then the identical dream? What was there about both that made her uneasy? Lying back and using the white ceiling as a screen, she pictured it all once more, from beginning cut to final concussion.

And then she knew. She sat up, counting as Timothy had. Five charges of dynamite. One, two three, four, five charges of dynamite. And only four detonations. One of them had misfired.

Leaping out of bed, she began to pace. Had Timothy gone back later and set off the fifth blast? Or had he been so distracted by his son's injury, he had forgotten the live charge? Debris from the earlier explosions had probably buried it.

Did it matter? If the fifth stick hadn't discharged, if it had waited in its rocky bed, under a lake, for at least eighty years, surely it would have deteriorated to harmlessness.

Whom did she know in civil engineering that she could call at half past midnight, and ask? No one. At a reasonable hour, Dr. Mahler would discuss it with her.

Hoping to establish whether the charge had been set off later, whenever Timothy had resumed work on his masterpiece, Charlie went to get the granite talisman to help guide her dreams. But she scarcely slept, frequently cracking an eyelid to monitor time's sluggish journey.

At 7:00 a.m., she got up and shuffled to the kitchen for coffee. She couldn't say whether it had been a waking or sleeping vision, but she had seen the dynamite dormant in the boulder, its fuse gently rocking in the water's current like an obscene tongue.

Dr. Mahler, chairman of the department of civil engineering and a staunch believer in out-of-body experiences, having once had one himself on an operating table, answered the phone with his usual gruff, "Well?"

"What do you want to know for?" he asked after Charlie had posed her question.

"I think this may have happened at a site a friend is excavating in Colorado. I want to warn him if there's danger."

"Well, wet, deteriorating dynamite is wildly unstable. And that early stuff was pretty unpredictable, even when it was fresh. It was usually something like forty percent nitroglycerin and sixty percent dope—wood pulp and salt. And it's true that a charge could be undetected for a number of years and some unsuspecting workman swinging his pick would get blown to kingdom come."

Charlie flinched. "So it's possible? After eighty years?"

"I doubt it. I doubt it. But anything's possible."

She thanked him and broke the connection, no closer to a decision than before.

At seven—Colorado time—she dialed Ross's home number and listened impassively to ten rings. He didn't answer at his office, either. Maybe she should try Brenda's place, Charlie thought sourly. She forced herself to wait a half hour before trying the two numbers again. Another half hour. Another.

At 9:00 a.m., his office phone clanked off the hook on ring five, and her heart leaped.

"Paul McCoy."

Both her heart and her head slumped with disappointment. "Hi, Paul. This is Charlie Yost. Is Ross around?"

"Hey, Charlie. How're you doing? No, Ross is up at the Sayers homestead trying to coax George Washington down the mountain."

"Does he come home nights? Weekends? I need to talk to him."

"I'm not sure when he'll be back. He and Evan have been camping up there for about a week."

"Paul, I need to get a message to Ross, and I hate to impose on you, but I can't think what else to do. This sounds a little crazy, probably—" She tried an unsuccessful laugh.

"What's the problem? If there's something I can do—"

"It's very likely, almost certain—" She tipped up her chin and began again. "There's a stick of dynamite that was never set off, a live charge, still in the base of the Washington boulder. On the north side, I think."

There was silence while he absorbed this. He asked gently, "Is this one of your psychic predictions?"

"No. I don't predict. I see the past, Paul. I know that explosive is there."

"Okay, suppose it is. After nearly a century, it must be a dud."

She nodded, eyes clenched. "Probably. I talked to an expert who says 'probably.' But Paul—" she had to swallow down the need to cry "—Paul, what if it is still capable of exploding? If Ross was hurt because I never warned him—"

"Okay, okay. I'll run up there this afternoon and let him know." He sounded less than enthusiastic.

"I'm really sorry to put you to this trouble."

"No problem. It's a nice day for a hike," he said with more warmth. "Don't worry about it."

"Thanks."

"Welcome."

Feeling not much better, she jogged to a convenience store three blocks south for milk, and stood inside the doorway a full minute trying to remember why she'd come. She wandered around the apartment, stared out windows, let full cups of coffee cool in front of her, picked things up and put them down again.

Mostly she imagined Paul swinging up the path to the lake site, hailing Ross, who'd be surprised and pleased to see him. After an exchange of banter, Paul would say, "Charlie—"

"Charlie?" What emotion would Ross feel, hearing her name?

"Charlie phoned this morning looking for you. She talked me into being a messenger service."

Ross would be completely intrigued now—she hoped.

"Charlie asked me to warn you there's a potentially volatile dynamite charge somewhere in the base of the statue."

And Ross's expression would change from interest to disappointment. He'd chuckle to cover his chagrin. "One of her psychic revelations, I assume?"

Paul would nod. "Could be true, you know."

"Sure. Thanks, Paul. You've done your duty."

He'd clap his hand on his friend's shoulder, they'd change the subject, and in a bit, Ross would go back to work, saddened by the memory of Charlie, pitying her for her beliefs. The insufferable, self-satisfied, opinionated—hunk!

And then she thought of the animals. If they were symbols, not to be taken literally, could the unexploded dynamite be symbolic of something, too? Not old, dead explosive, but—what?

She couldn't think. Ross's wonderful face floated in her mind's eye, and all Charlie could do was *feel*. Returning to the phone, she pawed through the directory, stabbed out a number and fidgeted while it rang.

"Midwest Travel."

"I need the earliest flight you can find from Chicago to Denver. One seat, round-trip. I'll probably be coming back twenty-four hours later."

The travel agent, taking Charlie seriously, found a nonstop jet leaving in one hour and ten minutes. There was hardly enough time to pack an overnight case and commandeer a taxi.

She collapsed into her no-smoking aisle seat, panting from a headlong sprint to the departure gate. The moment it was permitted, she reclined her seat and, using her shoulder bag for a pillow, slept the dreamless, restful sleep of the righteous.

ROSS LEANED on his shovel and wiped sweat from his face with his sleeve. The battered, wooden wheelbarrow beside him was full of rocky dirt to be trundled to the low end of the lake bed and dumped. Evan's stereo radio offended the thin, fresh air with rock and roll, but his pick rang steadily to the musical beat.

They'd been clearing out a trough around the statue's base to accommodate a gasoline-powered saw. A crane, scheduled to arrive Monday by helicopter, would lower the head to the homestead meadow. He rested the shovel against Washington's chest and hefted the lacerated handles of the barrow.

"Ross, ahoy!"

Ross squinted at the figure on the bank above, and motioned Evan to lower the radio volume. "Come on in, Paul—the water's so fine, it's invisible. There's an extra shovel."

Finding the natural rock stair steps Ross and Evans had been using, Paul joined them in the shadow of the head. This was the first time he'd seen it, and he made a circuit, one hand on the granite for balance in the litter of rock and loose dirt.

"Your granddad was quite a chiseler."

"Smile when you say that, pardner." Ross's arm and back muscles strained with the weight of the wheelbarrow as he prepared to shove it across the irregular basin.

Paul sauntered along beside him, hands clasped behind his back. "I had a phone call from Charlie today, or, actually, you did."

Ross misstepped into a hole and grunted. The barrow wobbled and then pushed on.

"She says—" Paul, obviously uncomfortable bringing this message to good old sensible Ross, cleared his throat. "She says there's a charge of unexploded dynamite in the statue. She's worried it could go off and hurt you. Or someone."

Ross thumped his burden down a few feet shy of his destination. "Ah, Paul, that woman's driving me crazy."

Paul frowned. "I didn't know you'd heard from her since she left Colorado."

"I haven't!" Ross's voice rose with aggrievement.

"Oh." He nodded understandingly.

Ross emptied the wheelbarrow with one vicious twist. "Do you know anything about dynamite?"

"Not much."

"It's not going to explode after all this time."

"She said that it probably wouldn't. But she wanted you to be aware of it."

"Thanks," Ross said curtly. Then he looked at his friend and repeated it, but this time he meant it.

SHE'D GAINED a couple of hours coming west. It was just a few minutes past 2:00 p.m. when the Boulder shuttle reached the Holiday Inn. Charlie reserved a room and snagged a taxi to the municipal airport where, she'd been advised, she could hire a helicopter.

A sign on the roof of the block building read Diamond Helicopter Service, and the logo on one parked alongside looked familiar. The office door squealed and led her into a bleak little room containing two scarred desks, three gray filing cabinets and a man reading a newspaper.

"Help you?" he asked without moving his feet off the desk.

"I need a helicopter to take me into the high country. Aren't you one of the gentlemen who airlifted a couple of friends and me from the Sayers Lake area after the May flood?"

He let his feet thud to the floor. "I remember you now. You look different with dry hair and a clean face." His eyes did a quick, objective inspection of the rest of her. "So what's the job?"

"Could you take me to the same place you picked us up that morning and wait while I deliver a message?"

"Sure. When do you want to do it?" He pulled a calendar toward him, making her heart sink.

"Now. As soon as possible."

"Mmm. Well, my partner's got the other chopper up on a sight-seeing party, due back at three. I could take you up then."

"That's the earliest?" She glanced out the grimy window at the helicopter drowsing in the yard.

"Afraid so. I don't like to leave the office unattended too long." He waved at his partner's chair. "Want to wait here?"

She didn't, but she had no choice. Wanting to discourage conversation, she brought a paperback out of her purse and watched the minute hand creep around her watch.

Three o'clock arrived, but the partner didn't. At five minutes after, her pilot, whose coveralls had Carl embroidered on the breast pocket, stood and stretched.

"Buddy shouldn't be much longer. I'll do the checklist on the whirlybird yonder, and we'll go whether he's here or not."

Sitting on a warm rock ledge, dangling their legs into the dry lake, Paul and Ross downed cans of beer. Dirt sprayed rhythmically from behind the statue, evidence of Evan's continued dedication.

"I never saw him work so hard," Paul marveled.

"It's a new philosophy he's trying called redemption through perspiration."

"He's still feeling guilty about Cid, huh? Wants to pay his debt by hauling rock?"

"He may decide we're at zero balance if he runs into that stick of dynamite," Ross remarked glumly.

"Look, since I'm here, I might as well toss a few shovelsful here and there." Paul stood and offered his hand.

Ross accepted the help, clutching his back like an old man. "Good, go right in. Admission's free." He shaded his eyes and shouted after Paul, "You'll get a bang out of it. Ha-ha."

THE HELICOPTER THREADED up the canyon, following a new gravel roadway. At the homestead turnoff, Charlie recognized Paul's dark sedan parked beside Ross's van. So he was, indeed, delivering her warning.

The beating rotors pulled them up the mountainside. Choke Creek sparkled below, once more a respectably slender line. The terrain looked vaguely familiar, like a face at a class reunion. Scoured of trees and bushes, it might have been some giant construction site.

Charlie recognized Whale Rock. Suddenly, she wanted to tell the pilot to turn back. Ever since this morning's decision to come to Colorado, she'd been anxiously eyeing clocks, mentally whipping the cars and aircraft that carried her to Ross. But now that she was within minutes of her goal, a different kind of apprehension swooped through her.

He'd think her a fool. He'd be embarrassed by her mission. He'd be angry. And whatever good memories he'd had of her would be smothered for all time by today's bad ones.

The helicopter floated to the level of the homestead meadow. No traces of a cabin remained. Like a tombstone, one severed ponderosa trunk marked the spot. A lime-green tent and a turquoise one had been pitched in the windbreak of the cliff.

Carl swayed over to yell in her ear. "You want down here or on the mesa yonder?"

Neither one! "Could we look at the lake bed," she shouted, "and then you can put me down here?"

Elevator-smooth, the helicopter brought them up the cliff, and higher, so that they looked into the steep-sided bowl that had been Sayers Lake. Ross was next to the statue with Evan and Paul, all of them gouging at the base with shovels or picks. A trick of the wind had camouflaged the rotors' approach. Now three faces tipped upward, like sunflowers tracking the sun.

"Hey." Carl patted her arm. "Isn't that one of the guys that was with you in the flood?"

She started to nod, assuming he meant Ross. But the pilot was gazing out the left side-window at the mesa. A lanky, dark-haired figure was just disappearing into the trailhead. Charlie caught a glimpse of Cid's single eyebrow beetling above his eyes.

Now what? she groaned to herself.

Carl peeled the helicopter sideways and they touched with the slightest of bumps in the center of the homestead meadow. Waiting impatiently till the motor died and the blades dipped motionless, she hit the ground running, scrambling up the path, seizing handholds of weeds and rocks. Behind her, someone else began to climb. She hoped it was Carl.

Rounding the narrow bend where she had once encountered Cid, Charlie half expected to find him looming, ready to pounce, but the trail was empty. She paused for five gasping breaths before forging on, her foreshortened shadow pointing the route. One final scramble and she was at the top, and there was Ross striding along the lake bank to meet her.

For the fifteen seconds it took for them to close the gap, Charlie was absolutely, unreservedly happy. Ross looked terrific—legs sheathed in dusty jeans, muscled arms below the rolled sleeves, tanned chest framed by the unbuttoned blue work shirt. His hair, longer than it had been in May, was bleached lighter by his labor in the sun, and his lean face was shadowed with several days' growth of beard. The blue eyes full of welcome suffused her with relief and love.

He wrapped her securely to his chest, and they held each other, not speaking.

Carl came puffing up the path, and they broke apart to let him by. He walked toward the edge of the lake.

Ross's arm encircled Charlie's shoulders and he drew her slowly in that direction, too, saying, "I thought you called Paul from Chicago this morning." His voice was as husky and warm as her memory had made it.

"I did. Then I decided to just run over and deliver the message in person."

"Emphasis on the word 'run,' apparently. You must have broken a few speed laws."

"Ross, I've been worried about you ever since you sent that chip of granite."

"I might have known you'd try to channel off it." He shook his head. "So okay, tell me about it."

They drifted to a stop as she described the blasting scene. She closed her eyes to recall the rich detail of weather, clothing, dog and the preparation and exploding of the dynamite. When she'd finished, she turned toward him and rested her hands on his waist, digging her thumbs through the belt loops.

"What do you think?"

He shrugged and rubbed a strand of her sweet-smelling hair between thumb and forefingers. "I don't think you saw the whole show." He patted her cheek, and Charlie's euphoria began to fade. "My grandfather wouldn't have left a live charge lying around. Nope. He set it off later."

"Okay, but—" She made an effort to lower her voice and smile. "What if the dynamite in my vision is symbolic of something else dangerous? In the same way as the animals representing the flood?"

"Charlie, I don't have time—" Ross made an effort also, and his voice and smile were as strained as hers. "How do you suggest we hunt for this danger?"

"I don't know. Maybe now that I'm here, I can get a clearer vision of it." She saw a smirk flicker across his lips and pulled away from him. "Okay, so you think that's dumb. What can I say to change your hermetically sealed mind?"

"Charlie," he began placatingly, "if I had time, I'd be happy to indulge your fears and explore the possibilities of unexploded dynamite or whatever. But heavy equipment rents by the day, big bucks. I promised the city I'd be ready for them first thing Monday. That means another full day of grubbing out rock."

Charlie snapped her fingers, mocking inspiration. "If you're worried about getting the job done, you should get Cid to help. He's skulking around here somewhere."

"I seriously doubt that."

"I saw him on the mesa!"

"You saw him," Ross muttered wearily.

Charlie threw up her hands and almost stamped her foot. "Saw with my two eyes. The way *normal* people do. Carl saw him, too," she added, pointing at the pilot, who'd gone exploring farther along the bank.

"Oh, God." Ross wiped a frustrated hand down his eyes, nose and mouth. "This is turning into a TV sit-com."

"Why isn't he in a hospital somewhere?"

"He's too good at mimicking sanity." Ross paced away from her, kicking pebbles out of his way. "He passed all the psychiatric tests. To put him behind bars, which isn't what he needs, you and I would have to press charges. Attempted murder, or whatever."

"Why do you suppose he came up here? Maybe he's the danger in my vision, him and his explosive personality."

She hadn't followed after Ross, and now a good eight feet separated them. No, a bad eight feet. She rubbed her arms, feeling bereft and depressed.

"I sure don't have time to play games with Cid. I'm going to ignore him and hope he goes away." Shoving his fists into his pockets, Ross scanned the pit of the lake.

And Charlie knew she'd lost him. His mind had taken up the next shovelful of rubble. She'd overstayed her welcome.

She shifted her gaze to the Washington head for what she knew, positively, was the last time. Paul had left his shovel biting the dirt beside a granite arm, and he was wending his way across the uneven floor to greet Charlie. Evan had tossed his pickax and work gloves aside to do the same, pausing to cough and spit and wipe his face with a red bandanna.

Staring down at the two men laboring toward her, their movements as deliberate as if they were traveling underwater, Charlie began to shake. She shut her eyes and saw light. When she opened them again, nothing had changed. The men were still coming, and Ross and Carl had not moved.

This time when she closed her eyes, there were numbers. Thirty, twenty-nine, twenty-eight, twenty-seven... "Ross," she breathed, wrenching her eyes open to search for him.

He was beginning to swing toward her, puzzled and concerned.

"Ross," she said louder. "Tell them to hurry."

He came to her and tried to take her in his arms, but she sidestepped away, and, body vibrating like a badly tuned car, she screamed toward the lake, "Run! Run!"

Both of them hesitated. Paul looked behind him, perhaps suspecting Evan of an imminent dirty trick. Charlie threw back her head and uttered a wordless, frustrated howl.

Thoroughly alarmed, Ross grasped her upper arm and dragged her into a rough embrace. Forcing her face into his chest with one hand spread behind her head, his troubled eyes looked past her shoulder and saw, on the horizon of the mesa, the spindly outline of a man, Cid, capering with his arms in the air, a victorious prize-fighter.

11

IT TOOK ROSS a moment to assimilate what he was seeing, and he wasted another second on an expletive. Then he was twisting around to shout at Paul and Evan to "Get out of there! Run!" Not waiting to confirm that they obeyed, he fell sideways, dragging Charlie with him, rolling over her, shielding her head with his chest and arms.

He felt her fingernails scrape his skin as she clutched his shirtfront. He heard the wheezing, rattling, bumping sounds of Paul and Evan climbing the lake bank. He smelled sweat and beer as they dropped down on either side of him, and Evan demanded, "What in hell's going on?"

"The other guy. The pilot. Is he away from the lake?" Ross asked, raising his head enough to look over Charlie's hair at the place he'd last noticed Carl.

"He's at the west end, gaping this way like he thinks we've all gone loony," Paul said.

There was absolute silence for two seconds.

The explosion jerked all four of them convulsively. It slammed against them as the kind of quick, loud noise that can skewer an eardrum, and bounced from rock to rock, losing volume.

As the thunder died away, a rain of dirt, pebbles and chunks of stone began. They squirmed deeper into the ground, wrapping their arms over their heads. The pelting debris stung their skin, bruised, drew blood.

When all noise and flagellation stopped, Ross listened to the hush before sitting up. Paul and Evan unfolded themselves and cautiously reconnoitered. Ross squinted first at the apparently empty mesa; then he stared down into Charlie's gleaming eyes. He opened his mouth to tell her something important, but couldn't find a beginning.

She waited expectantly, and when he didn't speak, she began, to her horror, to quietly weep.

"Are you hurt?" He scrambled off her, his voice thin with worry.

She shook her head, but he was already running his hands over her body, probing for the injury, and the sensations his investigation aroused in her yanked her upright, sputtering with laughter.

"Jesus," Evan was exclaiming over and over as he pushed himself up to stand beside Paul, both of them scrutinizing the lake.

Ross reached a hand to draw Charlie to her feet, and reluctantly they, too, turned to look at what they knew they'd see. Or wouldn't see.

The Washington head was gone. What was left of it, jagged chunks of granite, none bigger than a small refrigerator, littered the lake bottom. A pockmarked crater hissed with slithering gravel that was gradually filling it.

At the far end of the lake, Carl's face bobbed out of some bushes. He lurched to his feet and started to jog toward them, swinging his head frequently to examine the area of the blast.

"Jesus," Evan said unimaginatively. "What happened?"

Paul twisted to give Charlie a measuring look. "How did you know? The exact time?"

She threw a challenging glance at Ross and elevated her chin. "I saw the seconds ticking away. When I first saw them, we had thirty left."

Paul shook his head, mystified, amazed. A new thought occurred to him. "I thought you didn't do the future."

She considered. "I guess that means that when I saw thirty seconds, we really only had twenty-nine."

She and Paul shared a nervous laugh.

"Will somebody please tell me what's going on here?" Evan demanded.

Carl arrived, white, breathing like it hurt. "Did you folks mean to do that?" he panted.

"It was a bomb," Ross said, his jaw muscles clenching. "Courtesy of Cid Stillicidious."

"Why? How?" several asked together.

"Cid, like the Lord, moves in mysterious ways. He must have buried the charge last night, set to go off this afternoon." Ross reached for Charlie's hand and coaxed her to him, lacing his fingers through hers. Each pressure point radiated heat.

"What a shame," Paul commiserated. "A damned shame."

"Cid, we're going to get you for this!" Evan screeched at the sky and then put his back to the group, uncharacteristically self-conscious.

They shuffled their feet in numb indecision.

"At least now we don't have to lug that no 'count wheelbarrow home," Paul said.

"Jeeze, look." Evan gestured. "The rock's still smoking."

"Charlie, if it hadn't been for you—" Ross's fingers tightened in reflexive thankfulness that she was here, safe.

Paul asked, "So did your vision of Timothy's bad dynamite really represent Cid's hostile intentions?"

She shrugged and rubbed tear tracks from her cheeks with the back of her free hand. "Whatever it was doesn't matter. I just know I'm always going to respect my psychic hunches."

She threw Ross a sidelong, defensive look, but all he said was, "We all might as well go home. I've got to cancel the heavy equipment that was coming up here."

He glanced around the site, trying to find any intact possessions that would have to be collected. The lake basin seemed wider without the carved boulder island. He released Charlie to go to the edge for a last look. His foot rolled a softball-sized fragment, and he stooped to retrieve it.

The bomb had apportioned this piece five ragged sides and one smooth. No, not smooth. Timothy's authoritative chisel had converted the stone to a swirled button for a giant vest. Since it was too big for his pocket, Ross carried it in his hand as the five of them trooped down to the homestead campsite.

"Say, Ross." Paul stopped him as he began to pull out the first tent stake. "Evan and I will break up camp, and he can drive the stuff back to Boulder. You go on in the chopper with Charlie."

"I couldn't run out on you like that," Ross protested, although he cast a hopeful, sidelong glance at her.

"If Cid's still lurking around—" Charlie suggested regretfully.

"Yeah, we'd better go over everything carefully as we pack up. Make sure he didn't booby-trap anything else."

Spinning on his heel, Carl hurried to inspect the helicopter. The other men folded the tents, and Charlie collected their cooking supplies into a backpack.

"Okay if we send the baggage with you?" Ross interrupted Carl's concentration to ask.

"Sure, sure." He opened a compartment near the tail and helped stuff it full of canvas and nylon bundles.

"Evan and I will catch you later," Paul called, already entering the trailhead. Evan shrugged and held out a palm for the van key.

"We'll stick around till you're at the car park," Ross said. "To be certain you don't lose your way," he fabricated, giving Evan a fatherly slap on the back.

Evan showed Charlie a slow wink and trotted after Paul.

"That okay with you?" Ross asked the pilot belatedly.

"Up to the lady—it's her dime. How long will it take them to get there?"

"All downhill and nothing to carry and wondering if Cid's on their heels—I'd say ten minutes, easy."

"Ross," Charlie said, laughing, "it took us half a day to climb."

"Right. But we were easily distracted from the task at hand. By hunger, for instance. And hunger." The double entendre danced in his eyes as he brought her hand to his lips and gently bit it. "We'll walk over to the creek. You keep an eye on the copter," he told Carl.

They strolled to where Choke Creek tumbled cheerfully in what looked almost like its old bed. Impulsively, Charlie knelt to troll her fingers through the water.

"Well?" Ross said, eyebrows high.

She shook her head, grinning. "I see a glacier melting, drip by precious drip. And a deer spitting into the run-off."

Ross chuckled, captured her wet hand, and wiped it on his shirtfront. "I've missed you so much, Charlie."

"I've missed you, too."

He held her with his eyes as he lowered his face with tantalizing deliberateness to kiss her. His tender, warm lips tasted salty; his skin smelled like clean sheets drying in the sun.

He ended the kiss to murmur, "Soon as we get home, I have to do a few things. About the Washington head. And about Cid."

She nodded, burrowing her nose into the hollow of his throat.

"But after that," he went on, his voice like smooth syrup, "after that, you and I are going to be together. Alone. Very together."

Grudgingly extracting herself from his embrace, she smiled up at him, but her eyes glittered. "I don't think so, Ross. I'm sorry, but—" She inhaled the green scent of the mountain in a slow, ragged breath. "I don't think I could take another night of passion with you, knowing it's one of a kind."

"You mean because we—our relationship doesn't have a future?"

"Yes." She crossed her arms over the ache in her chest.

"Is that why you ran away a couple days early when you were here before?"

"Yes."

"You're saying it's better not to love then to love and lose?"

"Yes, yes, yes!" She put her back to him. "I'm sorry," she said bitterly. "I couldn't enjoy a one-night stand with you, Ross. I'd begin crying with the first kiss, and I wouldn't stop till the last."

"That would tend to put a damper on the lovemaking," Ross teased, his hand touching her spine and slipping under her hair to massage her neck.

"My plane leaves at eleven-something tomorrow morning." Charlie forced the words through an aching throat. "I think it would be best if we say goodbye this afternoon, when we get back to Boulder."

"No, damn it!" Ross twisted her around. His eyes burned into hers. "You're a hell of a lot stronger than that. You don't have to go to bed with me if you don't want to, but we're going to talk, by God. You can at least find the fortitude to have dinner with me and talk."

Wanting to emphasize his point, he shook her slightly, and continued glaring. Then he pulled her close for a quick, bone-grinding hug, whispering into her hair a piteous, "Please?"

THE HELICOPTER SAILED OFF the meadow and began to descend the mountain. It had been half an hour since Paul and Evan had disappeared down the trail, Ross having admitted that ten minutes was a trifle optimistic.

The clacking blades startled a pair of elk away from the creek, but otherwise there was no movement below, no sign of Cid. At the car park, Paul and Evan lounged on Paul's car, front bumper and hood respectively, drinking out of red cans. The two men waved and showed thumbs-up, and Carl pointed the helicopter down the road to Boulder.

Charlie and Ross stared out either side, his hand covering hers on the middle seat. A few miles down the canyon, Carl motioned at the road ahead. A black motorcycle with a black-garbed rider was making good time eastbound. As their shadow intersected his path, the cyclist raised his visored face and gestured rudely with a gloved finger.

Ross snorted. "That's got to be Cid."

"Is that the lowlife who trashed your statue?" Carl shouted.

"Looks like it," Ross shouted back. "Would you be willing to testify you saw him up on that mesa today?"

Carl nodded vigorously.

"How about you, Charlie?" Ross studied her. "You might have to come back to Colorado for a trial."

She, too, nodded, but her smile was bleak.

They sank to the grass at the Boulder airport near a twin helicopter; apparently Carl's partner had arrived safely after their departure. Ross took out a credit card to pay Carl, but Charlie insisted so fiercely that she would settle the bill, he let her. He didn't relish opening up any new areas of conflict.

They had to wait forty minutes for cab service, sitting without touching on Ross's rolled tents while the afternoon cooled toward evening. Little bursts of conversation flared now and then, about Mandy, Ross's aunt and mother, the weather. But for the most part they didn't speak, watching in opposite directions, thinking about each other.

When the taxi jounced into the airfield and rocked to a stop beside them, they struggled up, joints stiff, as much from tension as from inactivity.

"Where to, folks?" The young man didn't appear old enough to have a driver's license.

Ross gave his aunt's address; Charlie said, "Holiday Inn."

"I don't suppose—" Ross began but Charlie cut his request with a curt "No."

The motel was closer, or, at least, that's where the driver took them first. Ross stepped out on the sidewalk with her. "I'll call you as soon as I can. It might be a couple of hours till I can get away. We'll go someplace nice for dinner."

"Not too nice. I didn't bring my gold lamé."

She took a step toward the glass entry before Ross's hand anchored her wrist. "You won't run out on me this time, will you?" His grave face, tanned and whiskered and smudged with dirt, sent a shudder of desire through her.

"I'll be here when you call," she promised. When she walked away, her legs felt oddly unbalanced, as if she'd gotten someone else's by mistake.

"I NEED YOUR ADVICE on how to proceed here," Ross said, talking too fast and shutting his eyes against the sight of the kitchen clock's relentless second hand, anxious to get back to Charlie. He was talking to Detective Harshman, who'd taken his statement the night after the flood. "Louis Stillicidious detonated a time bomb at Sayers Lake where we were working. He could have killed five of us up there this afternoon."

"Where is he now, do you know?" The policeman's voice conveyed professional neutrality.

"Last we saw him, he was riding a motorcycle on his way back to Boulder from Sayers Lake."

More questions. More answers. Just when Ross thought he'd told everything he knew about the incident and Cid, Harshman said he'd come over right away.

Ross's splayed fingers raked his hair. "Can't you proceed from what I've given you? I have an important appointment now."

"If you want to press charges against Stillicidious, we need your signature on the complaint so we can issue a warrant."

"Yes, yes, I know. Okay, come over. If I don't answer right away, it might be because I'm in the shower."

Because it was Saturday, Ross had to call friends of friends to obtain a home phone number so he could cancel the order for machinery going up the mountain.

Finally, glancing again at the time, he phoned the Holiday Inn. The operator plugged him in to Charlie's number. As the line brayed, he imagined her coming to lift the receiver, her legs and feet bare, hair damp, skin smelling like wildflowers, slim fingers— She didn't answer. Stabbing the disconnect, he redialed.

"Holiday Inn."

"I'm trying to reach Charlie Yost. Would you ring her room again?"

After twelve rings, the operator broke in. "She isn't answering. Would you like to leave a message?"

He gave her his number, distracted by a different image of Charlie, in which she was fully dressed and speeding toward the Denver airport. Pacing the length of the kitchen, he delivered a vicious kick to the pantry door, which was imprudently ajar.

The phone rang and he lunged full-length for it. "Hello!"

"Hi. Ross?"

He pinched his eyes shut with relief. "Hi, Charlie."

"What's wrong? You sounded angry."

"Not angry, just frustrated. The police aren't through with me yet. There's a policeman coming over here to get my signature on a complaint, and he'll probably ask me every scintillating question that I already answered on the phone. And where were you when I called?"

"Taking a shower, but it's not polite to ask," she chided.

"I was too scared to be polite."

"Scared?"

"That you'd disappeared from my life again."

"I promised to stick around tonight. Don't you trust me?"

"No. Let me send a cab for you right away. If you're here when the officer arrives, you can sit in on the deposition. It'll be one hundred percent more pleasant if I can ogle you while I give it. And if he's gone by the time you get here, we can concentrate on more important matters."

She laughed. "You certainly would—I'm not dressed."

Ross smiled at the mouthpiece. "We'd better conclude this conversation. I feel some heavy breathing coming on. Get your own cab, but come quick. Okay?"

"Okay." She hung up without saying goodbye, to demonstrate she'd taken his exhortation seriously.

Ross showered, shaved and hustled into beige and gray shirt and slacks, coordinated with the efficiency of thirty years' experience and a limited wardrobe. Shoes in hand when the doorbell pealed, he stubbed his big toe on a table leg rushing to admit the police and, coincidentally, Evan, returning the van. Not letting anyone sit down, he signed the necessary papers and rushed everyone out before Charlie's taxi bumped up the driveway.

ROSS AND CHARLIE SAT in an east-facing window high above Boulder. Their waiter had brought them coffee, green salads, beautifully tender steaks and coffee, and now they rested elbows on the snowy tablecloth, lethargically awaiting dessert. A sound system hiding near the ceiling played "As Time Goes By."

Charlie performed an infinitesimal adjustment to the pink carnation gracing the center of the table. "You were right. This is a nice place to eat."

"It sure beats the can of soup I'd be warming up at Sayers Lake. I still can't believe it—the Washington carving gone, you here."

"What an inequitable trade!"

The waiter arrived with two wedges of cheesecake, flourished clean forks and exited with the inevitable, "Enjoy."

"You may have noticed I haven't returned your case of books," Ross said after the first taste.

"That's okay. I shouldn't have left you with the bother."

"No bother. The delay is, I've been reading the books."

Startled, she returned cup to saucer without taking a sip. "Why?"

"Isn't that what you brought them for? So I could learn about paranormal research?"

"Yes, but—" She picked up her fork and jabbed at the cheesecake. "You weren't much interested, as I recall."

"It's still not my favorite subject. I'm not convinced that dowsing or spoon bending or crystal power exists. But I'm willing to accept that what you do—psychic channeling or reading or whatever—has some scientific validity. Better minds than mine seem to be working on how such things work."

"Do you have to be able to explain it before you endorse it?" The question was posed in a deceptively soft tone.

Ross chewed and swallowed, planning his answer. "No. Because there are other phenomena we can't explain, either. Like—" He straightened his back, retrieved his fallen napkin, and avoided her serene eyes.

Like love, he wanted to say. He wanted to tell her he loved her. But blurting it out now would make her suspicious that his motive for such a confession was to lure her into his bed. Even though he very much wanted her in his bed! He did love her. He could admit it to himself now; he'd admit it to her, later.

"Like you said, gravity. And memory. And lots of other things," he finished lamely.

"You've really been boning up on the paranormal?" Charlie's mouth eased into a pleased curve. "I'm surprised you're willing to spend time on it. I know how busy you've been. When do you go to California?"

"Early August, but I could go sooner," he said. "No more Sayers tiara requiring my attention." He shook his head in bitter recollection. "What do you think you were channeling off, Charlie? What made you see the bomb?"

She shrugged. "I don't have to actually touch anything. Just being here was enough. Maybe—" Her eyes went blank, looking at the afternoon. "Maybe the dust on your shirt." Smiling, she added, "You looked very Indiana Jones-ish up there, all disheveled and active."

"And you looked like an angel dropping out of the sky."

"Does this mean I finally did something you're willing to call extrasensory?"

He swirled his coffee cup before draining it. "Unless you planted that bomb yourself, I don't see any way you could have known it was there." He narrowed his eyes at her. "If I had to testify, I'd swear on the Bible that Charlie Yost is psychic. But it'll take me a while to come to grips with the reality of ESP. I can't accept it without a struggle."

"I wouldn't expect you to. The concept is so bizarre. Only an idiot would embrace it uncritically."

"I know I said things that hurt you, Charlie. I'm sorry."

Basking in his penitent words and contrite expression, Charlie jumped at the sudden voice above her head. "More coffee?"

"I think I'll have my next cup at lower altitude. Okay with you?" Ross pinned her with a meaningful look.

Feeling like a skier plunging out of the ski-jump gate, she nodded once.

"So," Ross said, thumping a mug onto his aunt's table in front of Charlie. "Are you satisfied that I've changed for the better? That my mind has swung open a notch?"

"Of course, I'm pleased. Provided it isn't a temporary disposition." Coffee steam wafted under her chin, soothing her with its warmth and aroma.

"That's up to you."

"What do you mean?"

"I mean I'm really getting into this paranormal stuff. I could devote some time to it, maybe even set up experiments in it that would tie in with my history interests. But only if you're there to help. If you aren't around, I wouldn't care that much about it." He dropped into a chair opposite her and draped his arm nonchalantly across its back.

"I'm afraid I don't follow. What do you have in mind?" Charlie sipped at coffee that was too hot to sip.

"Before you say no, Charlie, think about it. Come to California with me."

The pain in her tongue spread to her chest. "Just 'come to California?' You'll have to be more specific than that."

"Okay. Come to California with me in August."

She shifted in the chair, annoyed with his flippancy.

He'd been flippant, he knew, to protect himself in case she rejected his proposition. Sterner measures seemed to be required. "All right, Charlie, here it is. No holds barred."

She waited expectantly.

"We should be together." He looked at the ceiling for inspiration. "I want to live with you."

Her face reminded him of his mother's when he'd had to confess some boyish infraction—skeptical and a little disappointed. He threw up his hands in complete capitulation. "Okay, I love you. I love you and I want to marry you." His chin jutted out belligerently as he braced himself for her reaction.

The smile began in her eyes, spread to her mouth, relaxed her body, and its contagion reached across the table, filling him with hope.

She touched her temple with the fingertips of one hand while the other hand pretended to fan. "You certainly know how to sweet-talk a woman, Dr. Davies."

Pushing back her chair, she rose and sauntered over to him. Ross scraped his own chair sideways, but she stopped him from standing by settling herself down on his lap. Resting her arms across his shoulders, she kissed him with several light, chaste touches of her satiny mouth. Then she hugged him hard, and he felt a suspicious wetness on his neck.

"Uh, am I right to assume your answer's yes?" he hazarded.

She bobbed her head. "I love you," she whispered into his left ear.

"All right!" he growled. "Would you care to shake hands on it? Or do something even more symbolic?" He stroked her hair.

"Could we—would you just hold me for a little while?"

And that was enough, their arms around each other in the exquisite tenderness of a man and a woman securely in love.

It wasn't enough for long. Ross's fingers began to explore her back, hips, bare legs, sliding over the curves and hollows of her body. His hand glided up from the crook of one knee, under the hem of her dress, along the smooth outer edge of her thigh to the elastic edge of her briefs. He traced this barrier forward between her legs, across the delicate bridge of bone between inner leg and pelvis.

She changed position, and he tipped back his head and laughed his joy, because she hadn't moved protectively—she'd made access easier. He slipped two fingers under the elastic and drew his knuckles down the secret, moist center. She clutched his shoulders and moaned against his neck. He nuzzled her face into position for a leisurely, passion-stirring kiss.

The telephone's scream made both of them jump. Ross half carried her with him to go answer it, and she sagged against him, knees unsteady with desire.

"Dr. Davies? Detective Harshman. Thought you'd want to know that Louis Stillicidious led two of our patrol cars on a high-speed chase that ended in him losing control of his cycle. On Flagstaff Road. We have him in custody."

"Thanks," Ross said and quietly put up the receiver, resolving, as he disengaged the bell, not to let Cid spoil this moment for Charlie. He'd tell her later.

One arm supporting her waist, Ross's free hand toyed with the collar of her dress. "This is the same blue dress you were wearing the first time I saw you."

"I discovered I could wash it and wear it more than once," she whispered, eyes shut.

He undid one button, and his knuckles brushed the warm curve of breast above her bra. "I wanted to do this the first time I saw you." He worked the next button free. The pads of his fingers slid down the valley between her breasts.

"Our friendship would have gotten off to a very shaky start if you had," she gasped.

A third button prized free. A fourth. Ross spread the bodice wide to admire the golden expanse of skin above and below the white, lace-trimmed bra.

Charlie glanced down at herself and, suddenly shy, hid her cleavage by pressing it into Ross's chest. "Your aunt's kitchen isn't the place for this."

"Sure it is. I'm feasting my eyes on you before I start to nibble on the choicest parts."

"No, Ross," she admonished. "People on the street can see in."

"We'll make it a progressive dinner, then. I've had my appetizer—now let's move on to the main course."

Sweeping her up, he carried her triumphantly into the hall toward his room.

Charlie rested her head against his neck, feeling very feminine and protected in his arms. He went through the bedroom door sideways and lowered her feet to the floor beside his quilt-covered double bed. When he released her shoulders, she swayed, drunk with anticipation.

He steadied her by gripping her upper arms, and she tilted her face to his kiss. It began as a quiet, testifying touch of flesh to flesh, and it built and intensified into a tangle of mouths and bodies.

Charlie clung to Ross's waist, feeling his need swelling between them, desperate to lie down with him. Forcing her backward to the bed, his sinewy arms controlling her descent, he leaned over her to clumsily unfasten the remaining buttons and rake the dress away from her. Pausing to contemplate the expanse of skin he'd laid bare, Ross inserted a tentative finger at the center of her bra and tugged. The clasp sprang loose with a faint pop. Charlie held her breath, legs aching with tension, and sighed in disappointment when his hovering hand moved away.

Then he pulled her bikini briefs down slowly, sawing them past her hips and knees. Again, he didn't touch what he'd exposed. She gritted her teeth.

The bed jiggled as he pushed away from it, backed into the room and shrugged out of his own clothes.

Though his mouth smiled, the intensity of his eyes didn't waver. He came toward the bed, but her welcoming reach fell short as he detoured to the bedside table. He stirred through the drawer, searching for the protection that, even in the midst of his desire for her, he'd remembered.

"Wait," she said, hitching higher on the bed to caress the bare skin he was about to cover. While he became harder in her hand, she said, "We don't need anything tonight. I don't want anything between us. I can't imagine ever getting close enough to you."

Lying down beside her, sighing, he began a systematic tour of her, touching, licking, sucking and nipping, inch by sensitive inch. With every nerve ending tingling, she twisted under his mouth, deliriously out of control.

Ross rolled onto his back, dragging her over him like a blanket. "Raise your hips. Yes, there," he said choreographing their union.

On her knees above him with his hands holding her wrists on either side of his head, Charlie shuddered as Ross rose to meet her. Filled with his desire, she rocked slowly. He lifted his head to tongue one nipple, and then he pulled back to dry it with a drawn-out breath, jolting her as if a live wire ran directly from breast to groin.

Her head snapped forward, spilling her hair in a curtain around them. For a few seconds, Charlie throbbed, suspended on the rim, and then she toppled into a joyous, vibrating climax. Ross's palms against her hips ground her onto him, and, to the accompaniment of her cries of satiation, he shimmied past the point of no return.

Eventually they lay still. Their panting subsided. His hand affectionately rubbed her back.

"Ahhh, Charlie," he marveled, abruptly serious. "I'm dreaming. You're too good to be true. You're a psychic vision I'm having because I concentrated on you so much."

"I thought of you, too," she confessed, tracing his jaw with a thumb. "Trying to forget you was like trying not to breathe."

"I've found the moral in that creek pebble, the one that dries up brown when it's out of the water. My life would be like that, Charlie, dull and ugly, without you. You make me sparkle."

Hugging him fiercely, she answered past the lump in her throat, "I came to Colorado hunting for treasure—something beautiful and old and rare." She leaned away to smile into his eyes. "And here you are."

He laughed, but before he could protest, she rushed to say, "Two out of three ain't bad!"

Harlequin Intrigue

QUID PRO QUO

Racketeer King Crawley is a man who lives by one rule: An Eye For An Eye. Put behind bars for his sins against humanity, Crawley is driven by an insatiable need to get even with the judge who betrayed him. And the only way to have his revenge is for the judge's children to suffer for their father's sins....

Harlequin Intrigue introduces Patricia Rosemoor's QUID PRO QUO series: #161 PUSHED TO THE LIMIT (May 1991), #163 SQUARING ACCOUNTS (June 1991) and #165 NO HOLDS BARRED (July 1991).

Meet:

Sydney Raferty: She is the first to feel the wrath of King Crawley's vengeance. Pushed to the brink of insanity, she must fight her way back to reality—with the help of Benno DeMartino in #161 PUSHED TO THE LIMIT.

Dakota Raferty: The judge's only son, he is a man whose honest nature falls prey to the racketeer's madness. With Honor Bright, he becomes an unsuspecting pawn in a game of deadly revenge in #163 SQUARING ACCOUNTS.

Asia Raferty: The youngest of the siblings, she is stalked by Crawley and must find a way to end the vendetta. Only one man can help—Dominic Crawley. But will the son join forces with his father's enemy in #165 NO HOLDS BARRED?

Don't miss a single title of Patricia Rosemoor's QUID PRO QUO trilogy coming to you from Harlequin Intrigue.

HARLEQUIN
Romance

**This June, travel to Turkey
with Harlequin Romance's**

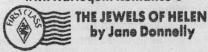

**THE JEWELS OF HELEN
by Jane Donnelly**

She was a spoiled brat who liked her own way.

Eight years ago Max Torba thought Anni was self-centered—
and that she didn't care if her demands made life impossible
for those who loved her.

Now, meeting again at Max's home in Turkey, it was clear he
still held the same opinion, no matter how hard she tried to
make a good impression. ''You haven't changed much, have
you?'' he said. ''You still don't give a damn for the trouble you
cause.''

But did Max's opinion really matter? After all, Anni had no
intention of adding herself to his admiring band of female
followers....

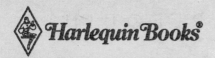

GREAT NEWS...

HARLEQUIN UNVEILS NEW SHIPPING PLANS

For the convenience of customers, Harlequin has announced that Harlequin romances will now be available in stores at these convenient times each month*:

Harlequin Presents, American Romance, Historical, Intrigue:

>   May titles: April 10
>   June titles: May 8
>   July titles: June 5
>   August titles: July 10

Harlequin Romance, Superromance, Temptation, Regency Romance:

>   May titles: April 24
>   June titles: May 22
>   July titles: June 19
>   August titles: July 24

We hope this new schedule is convenient for you.

With only two trips each month to your local bookseller, you'll never miss any of your favorite authors!

*Please note: There may be slight variations in on-sale dates in your area due to differences in shipping and handling.

HDATES-RR

*Applicable to U.S. only.

You'll flip . . . your pages won't!
Read paperbacks *hands-free* with

Book Mate · I

The perfect "mate" for all your romance paperbacks
Traveling • Vacationing • At Work • In Bed • Studying
• Cooking • Eating

Perfect size for all standard paperbacks, this wonderful invention makes reading a pure pleasure! Ingenious design holds paperback books OPEN and FLAT so even wind can't ruffle pages— leaves your hands free to do other things. Reinforced, wipe-clean vinyl-covered holder flexes to let you turn pages without undoing the strap . . . supports paperbacks so well, they have the strength of hardcovers!

Pages turn WITHOUT opening the strap.

SEE-THROUGH STRAP

Reinforced back stays flat.

Built in bookmark

BOOK MARK

BACK COVER HOLDING STRIP

10 x 7¼ . opened.
Snaps closed for easy carrying, too.

Available now. Send your name, address, and zip code, along with a check or money order for just $5.95 + .75¢ for delivery (for a total of $6.70) payable to Reader Service to:

Reader Service
Bookmate Offer
3010 Walden Avenue
P.O. Box 1396
Buffalo, N.Y. 14269-1396

Offer not available in Canada
*New York residents add appropriate sales tax.

BM-GR

Back by Popular Demand

Janet Dailey
Americana

A romantic tour of America through fifty favorite Harlequin Presents® novels, each set in a different state researched by Janet and her husband, Bill. A journey of a lifetime in one cherished collection.

In June, don't miss the sultry states featured in:

Title # 9 - FLORIDA
Southern Nights
#10 - GEORGIA
Night of the Cotillion

*Available wherever
Harlequin books are sold.*

JD-JR